"What is your question?"

Alison's voice was pensive.

Philip hesitated, as if uncertain whether to proceed. "When I came to your house, you asked if I were a lord and I told you I was not. I thought I heard you say 'good,' as you turned away. Why?"

"Because I did not like you," she muttered, sure that she was crimson to the roots of her hair.

"I see. I did not precisely behave so as to ingratiate myself," he said wryly. "May I hope to be forgiven?"

"I like you very well now," she hastened to assure him. "Indeed, I do not know when I have enjoyed anything so much as driving in the Park this afternoon."

"Thank you, Miss Larkin. You mean since meeting your first lord, I collect?"

Alison laughed merrily even though she was not at all sure he was joking.

Books by Carola Dunn

HARLEQUIN REGENCY ROMANCE
25—A SUSCEPTIBLE GENTLEMAN
39—A POOR RELATION

A LORD FOR MISS LARKIN

CAROLA DUNN

Harlequin Books

TORONTO • NEW YORK • LONDON
AMSTERDAM • PARIS • SYDNEY • HAMBURG
STOCKHOLM • ATHENS • TOKYO • MILAN

Published June 1991

ISBN 0-373-31152-4

A LORD FOR MISS LARKIN

CHAPTER ONE

WITH A SIGH of satisfaction, Alison closed the marbled covers of Mrs. Kitty Cuthbertson's latest novel. Curled in the corner of the shabby sofa, so faded its colours were indistinguishable, for a few moments she let her imagination drift through marble palaces and dark, sinister, ruined abbeys. How romantic it would be to have a handsome young lord swooning at one's feet! Or better (suggested her practical streak), simply kneeling in adoration.

The grey rain drummed down outside the window. In the grate the meagre fire gave a last despairing flicker and died. Alison shivered, uncurled, set the borrowed volume carefully on the occasional table by the parlour door and picked up her feather duster.

The huge black dog sprawled on the hearth rug raised his head to watch tolerantly as she flitted about the room, making mysterious passes at shelves and picture frames and the one remaining Dresden shepherdess on the mantel. The whims of humans were inexplicable. He lumbered to his feet and padded over to the window. The sill was just the right height for his chin, and even though it was raining there was always the possibility that a cat might venture to dash across the street.

What he did not know was that at present Alison was not a romantic heroine but a fairy godmother. With her magic wand she was turning everything in the room into gold. Then she would buy a splendid gown for her dear goddaughter, Miss Alison Larkin, who would go to a ball and meet—well, a prince was too much to expect, and even a duke's son seemed a lot to ask for, although judging by Mrs. Meeke's novels they were two a penny. Alison would be satisfied with an earl or a viscount, or even a mere baron.

She gave an extra whisk of the duster to the picture over the mantelpiece. Looking at the portrait was almost like gazing in a mirror—curly black hair, brilliant blue eyes and delicate, pixielike features. When the likeness was painted Mama had been nineteen, Alison's present age, and Papa not much older. She did not remember them.

She curtsied, blew a kiss and turned away.

"Midnight! Stop pressing your nose against the glass, you naughty boy. I just cleaned it yesterday," she said in fond exasperation. She pushed the amiable monster out of the way and rubbed at the smear with the holland apron that swathed her navy-blue stuff gown. "I believe the rain is letting up. I'll take you out but you'll have to stay in the kitchen to dry off afterwards, whatever Aunt Cleo may say."

"Whuff," he agreed, the deep voice echoing from his barrel chest.

He followed her to the door, tail waving. She just managed to catch the book as the black plume swept it off the table. Letty would never lend her another novel if any harm came to this one.

She opened the door a crack and peeked out.

"All clear. Come on quickly now, boy."

The parlour door was barely closed behind them when three small white terriers dashed along the passage from the kitchen. Their welcome was as vociferous as if they had not seen Alison for a week, instead of the three hours since she had given them their breakfast. Midnight stood patiently as they bounced around and under him.

"Is the parlour door closed, Alison?" An angular figure in a grey gown and plain white cotton cap was trotting after the dogs. "Down, Goose."

"Yes, Aunt Di. I've no wish to spend the rest of the day brushing white hairs off the chairs."

"I'm sure I don't know why Polly makes such a fuss. After all, she spends half her time covered in mud."

"That is why she likes to be tidy the other half," Alison explained, not for the first time. Aunt Polly's insistence that she be allowed one room where she could sit without her clothes gathering dog hairs, the only time she ever stood up for her rights, was a constant bone of contention.

"I was going to see if Cleo happens to have a pot of tea on hand. Such a nuisance, my last pen broke when I was half-way through the accounts."

"I'm about to take Midnight out. Shall I buy you some quills?" She moved towards the kitchen, followed by the dogs and her aunt.

"A shocking price they are these days, but I fear I cannot manage without. Yes, dear, buy me half a dozen. Or perhaps I should try one of those newfangled steel pens?"

The front door knocker sounded and Alison turned back to answer it. On the doorstep stood a smartly dressed lad, somewhat damp, with a small package in his hand.

"Letter fer Larking," he announced.

"Larkin. Thank you. Wait a moment and I shall get you a penny for your trouble."

The package disappeared behind his back. "Sixpence, more like, miss. I come all the way from the City in the rain an'..."

Before he could finish his sentence, an urchin who had been dawdling on the other side of Great Ormond Street dashed across, whipped the letter from his grasp and presented it to Alison with a smirk on his freckled face and a clumsy bow.

"'Avin' a spot o' trouble wiv 'im, miss? I'll sort 'im out fer ya."

Alison grinned at him. "Thank you, Tarry Joe, everything is fine now. Go round to the kitchen and tell Aunt Cleo I said to give you a penny, for you have saved me five."

The boy nodded and slipped away. The messenger snorted in disgust, put his hands in his pockets and sauntered off whistling with an air of nonchalance. Alison closed the front door and read the direction on the package.

It was from India, carried by Captain Barlow of the *Merry Maiden.*. Alison picked up her skirts in one hand and ran towards the kitchen, crying, "Aunt Di, there's a letter from Aunt Zenobia!"

The terriers decided she wanted a game and gamboled about her feet, nearly tripping her. Midnight sat by the closed kitchen door regarding her hopefully, the tip of his tail swishing gently on the flagstones. She rubbed his huge head as she passed.

"Sorry, boy, you will have to wait. Sit, Flake, Goose, Drop. Stay!"

The terriers obeyed, with a reproachful look that made her laugh. She slipped into the warm kitchen, fragrant with the odour of baking, and closed the door firmly again behind her.

All three of her aunts were sitting at the well-scrubbed white wood table, sipping tea from cheap china cups. Aunt Cleo, plump and rosy-cheeked, reached for the teapot as Alison entered and poured a fourth cup.

"Who was it, dear?" she asked.

"A messenger, with a letter from Aunt Zenobia." She set the package in front of Aunt Polly and sat down beside her.

As the eldest of the sisters, Polly Larkin was entitled to be the one to open the letter. A vague-looking woman with wisps of grey hair escaping from her cap, she poked the package with a nervous expression.

"Oh, dear. Di, will you read it?" she said pleadingly, just as everyone expected.

Warming her hands on her cup of tea, Alison waited impatiently as the ritual proceeded. Aunt Di found her steel-rimmed spectacles suspended round her neck, as always. Aunt Cleo provided a sharp knife to slit the seal, warning her sister to be careful not to damage the contents. Aunt Zenobia Winkle had not been heard from in two years, but they all remembered the bright-hued silk scarves that had been enclosed with her last letter, though they had been sold long since to buy coals.

Eyes widened as four pairs of gold earrings emerged from their tissue paper wrappings.

"I shall buy a goose!" exclaimed Aunt Cleo. "I did want a goose to roast for Christmas, but better late than never."

Alison let out her breath in a long, silent sigh. Of course, they would have to be sold. With a reverent fingertip she touched the nearest one, a delightful dangling creation shaped like a pagoda.

"They are a bit *flashy*," said Aunt Di, doubtfully. "Do you think anyone will buy them?"

"Of course. There is a certain type of female who *likes* to be flashy."

Alison was about to request elucidation of this fascinating comment when Aunt Polly's timid voice was heard.

"Surely the gold alone must be worth something?"

"Quite right, Polly." Cleo patted her hand. "I daresay there will be enough to buy us each a new dress."

Visions of silks and satins danced before Alison's eyes. Resolutely she banished them. A sprig muslin for spring would do nicely. "What does the letter say, Aunt Di?" she asked.

Her aunt unfolded the sheet of paper with some trepidation. Zenobia's communications were generally full of incomprehensible and unpronounceable memsahibs and howdahs and chukkers and tiffins.

"My goodness!" she gasped. "Mr. Winkle is gone to his reward and Zenobia is coming home at last. And this letter must have been delayed—she expects to arrive at the end of January. She may be here any day!"

A stunned silence was broken by a knocking at the garden door. Cleo answered it, gave Tarry Joe his penny and bustled back.

"Well, no time for sitting about," she grumbled. "It's past time I started on the pastry for the meat pies. Clear the table for me, please, Alison dear."

While Alison piled the crockery in the scullery sink, Polly vanished in her silent way, presumably returning to her potting shed in the back garden. Di and Cleo

held a brief consultation, then Di gathered up the earrings and wrapped them carefully in the tissue.

"Shall I take them to the pawnbroker's?" Alison
enquired. "I promised Midnight a walk anyway."

"No, dear." Di glanced at her sister for support.
"We think these should go to a proper jeweller, on
Oxford Street. Wear your best pelisse and do not take
Midnight into the shop, whatever you do."

Alison almost skipped down Southampton Row,
Midnight padding along at her side. There was no
knowing what changes Aunt Zenobia's homecoming
might bring. At the very least it meant a new face, and
probably exciting stories about life in India. Perhaps
she would bring a few presents that did not have to be
sold to pay the bills.

The house must be turned out from top to bottom in
preparation for her arrival. With luck the proceeds
from the sale of the earrings would be enough to hire
one or two women from the tenements on the south
side of Great Ormond Street to help with the heavy
work. Mrs. 'Arris, their regular cleaner, would know
whom to ask.

When she came out of the jeweller's shop with what
seemed like a small fortune in her reticule, Alison was
glad of Midnight's escort. He might be the mildest
creature on the face of the earth, but his size was
enough to discourage pickpockets. All the same she
had a nervous moment when she came face to face with
a ragamuffin as she turned the corner into Tottenham
Court Road. Then she recognized him.

"Hello, Squeak. Have you sold all your flowers already?"

"Yes, miss." His high voice explained his nickname. "Miss Polly don't 'ave much this time o' year,

jist a few snowdrops. Miss Cleo's pies is better, people likes 'ot pies when it's cold an' wet out.''

Alison smiled and nodded and went on her way. Midnight glanced back, but if he saw the skinny urchin trailing after them he apparently thought him harmless, for he did not notify his mistress.

The next several days were frantically busy. The last pair of curtains had just been rehemmed, to hide the tattered edges, and rehung, when a vigorous rat-a-tat-tat resounded through the house.

Alison rushed to the front door, followed by a yapping tide of white fur. A postilion stood there in the dusk, his hand raised to knock again. In the street, a post-chaise piled high with trunks and boxes swayed alarmingly as a large, round, scarlet object emerged from its interior. On one side of the carriage door a tall, well-built gentleman lent a hand; on the other a tiny figure swathed in white hovered anxiously.

The scarlet object put out a foot, heel foremost, and cautiously felt for the ground. Another foot followed. The object turned around. For the most part the front view differed little from the back, but it was topped by a beaming face with a white turban concealing one eye.

The gentleman hurriedly straightened the turban. Its wearer glanced up the steps to the front door.

"You must be little Alison," boomed Aunt Zenobia Winkle.

Alison curtsied. "Yes, ma'am. Welcome home."

Once set in motion, the India merchant's widow was remarkably light on her feet. She swept up the steps and half-smothered Alison in a musky-scented embrace. The terriers, after one sniff, sneezed and retreated, overcome by an excess of patchouli.

Alison managed to extricate herself before she too sneezed. The rest of the aunts had appeared meanwhile. As they greeted their long-lost sister, Alison turned back to the street, where the gentleman and the tiny, dark-skinned maid were directing the unloading of vast quantities of luggage. Fortunately, Squeak and his brother and Tarry Joe turned up to assist the postilion and coachman in carrying trunks and boxes and portmanteaux into the hall.

Aunt Zenobia introduced the gentleman as Mr. Ralph Osborne, "poor Winkle's partner and my business wallah." Alison regarded him with curiosity. In the dimly lit hall he appeared distinguished, handsome even, with a brown face and light blond hair. His voice, when he politely refused refreshment and said he must repair to his hotel, was deep and calm.

Alison was delighted when he promised to call next day to see how Mrs. Winkle went on. She saw him to the door. As he bid her farewell, he tipped his hat and the light of a nearby street lamp fell full upon his face. Closing the door, she sighed in disappointment: alas, the handsome Mr. Osborne was quite old.

She helped Aunt Cleo carry the tea tray into the parlour. Aunt Polly was mending the fire. Aunt Zenobia, sunk with an air of permanence into a sagging armchair, gazed about the shabby room in dismay.

"Deary me, this will never do!" she said.

Seeing an offended retort spring to Aunt Di's lips, Alison intervened. "Did you have a pleasant voyage, Aunt Zenobia?"

"Why yes, child, number one chow-chow. I did think it might be kutcha, for I couldn't expect a dashing young wallah like Ralph to dance attendance on an old mem-sahib like me. Then I had a pukka notion. My

old friend Mrs. Colonel Bowditch was talking of staying in Madras after the colonel died because she don't
like travelling. I knew she'd be happier at home so I
told her straight, I said . . ."

Listening with half her attention to the tale of Mrs.
Colonel Bowditch's sufferings on the voyage round the
Cape, Alison pondered the description of Ralph
Osborne as a "dashing young wallah." Perhaps his life
in a hot climate had made him appear older than he
really was. He had no title, but after all she had never
really expected to meet anyone with a title anyway.
Certainly he was much to be preferred to the apothecary's assistant with the constant drip on the tip of his
nose, her most persistent suitor.

With a start, she realized Aunt Di was speaking to
her.

"Alison, pray show Zenobia to her chamber."

She sat on Aunt Zenobia's bed while the abigail
("my ayah," said her aunt) helped her mistress change
from the scarlet sari embroidered in gold into an
equally spectacular peacock blue with a tasselled
fringe. The open trunk offered a tantalizing peek of
fabulous silks in every colour of the rainbow. Resolutely Alison turned her eyes away.

"Have you known Mr. Osborne for long, Aunt?"
she asked.

"Nearly twenty years, my dear. He came out at seventeen as an apprentice and mighty well he's done for
himself. I told him straight, I said, it's time to go home
and settle down with a wife, so here he is."

Concentrating on her mental arithmetic, Alison
missed her aunt's sly glance. Seventeen—nearly twenty
years—why, he was at least five and thirty.

"Dinner's ready," said Aunt Di, popping her head around the door.

As usual they ate in the kitchen, the warmest room in the house.

"Deary me, this will never do!" exclaimed Aunt Zenobia, eyeing with dismay her plate of stew, which consisted of a few small bits of yesterday's mutton eked out with a great quantity of potatoes.

"I did not know you would arrive today," said Aunt Cleo in self-defense. "I shall get a goose tomorrow."

"This is delicious, Aunt Cleo," Alison assured her.

"First chop," said Aunt Zenobia doubtfully, "though I'm used to spicier food. But that is not what I meant at all. My dears, I never dreamt you were all living like untouchables. This will never do."

"I don't know what an untouchable is, but we do what we can." It was Aunt Di's turn to spring to the defense of the household. "Polly grows flowers to sell, and Cleo's biscuits and pies are very popular. And I myself have had some success with my terriers. It's just that the annuity Hector left Alison was not very large, you know."

"Since our brother was still alive when I married Winkle and went off to India, I had no notion. But though he was sadly slow about it, Winkle did become a nabob in the end. I shall set everything to right, I promise you."

"Alison needs some pretty dresses," said Cleo gruffly. Aunt Polly nodded agreement.

"Aunt Polly ought to have a fire in her bedroom," Alison put in eagerly. "Her rheumatism is shockingly troublesome in the mornings."

Aunt Zenobia laughed merrily. "There will be fires in every room," she assured them. "And as for pretty gowns, why, I mean for Alison to have a pukka Season!"

Four pairs of eyes gazed at her in astonishment. Aunt Di was the first to find her voice.

"A Season! I am sure dear Alison deserves it, but we have no connexions in the best society. Remember the child's grandfather refused to acknowledge her."

Alison was not discouraged. From the miles of flamboyant silk wound about Aunt Zenobia's generous form to the curious brassy red hue of her hair under the turban with its sapphire aigrette, the nabob's widow was clearly a fairy godmother in disguise. At any moment she would wave her wand.

"I shall hire a chaperon for Alison, an impoverished lady who moves in the first circles, a real burra beebee. Mrs. Colonel Bowditch will know just where to look. When you have as many lakhs of rupees as I do," said Mrs. Winkle grandly with an airy wave of her beringed hand, "nothing is impossible."

CHAPTER TWO

"I CANNOT LIKE IT," said Philip Trevelyan. "I wish you will marry me."

Lady Emma Grant cast an affectionate glance at his serious face, intent on guiding his team through the busy traffic of Oxford Street. "No, Philip, I will not. You are only nine and twenty, far too young to despair of falling in love one day."

"Highly unlikely. You are the only female I know who does not bore me intolerably."

"I cannot think that sufficient grounds for marriage! You know I do not mind acting as a chaperon for hire. It is a respectable occupation for a widow and allows me to enjoy the Season while assuring my independence."

"But Great Ormond Street! None but Cits live in that part of Town. At least your previous protégées have been of impeccable birth."

"I need not accept Miss Larkin if I do not care for her," she said tranquilly. "Besides, Mrs. Winkle's letter hints at blue blood in the background somewhere."

Her companion snorted. "Still worse. Some noble lecher's by-blow, no doubt. Is her name truly Winkle?"

"The aunt's, yes. Zenobia Winkle—did you ever hear the like? Her letter says that she is a nabob's widow and well able to buy an abbey. To tell the truth, I am all agog to meet her though I may not accept her niece.''

Mr. Trevelyan swung the tilbury into Southampton Row, then turned right and found himself in a blind court. Though this provided an opportunity to display his driving skill, his mood was not improved when, after asking the way, he found himself driving down a narrow street lined with drab tenements. Ragged children played in the gutters and a slatternly woman shouted something at them, probably rude but fortunately incomprehensible.

"Cits, I said,'' he remarked bitterly. "It begins to look more as if you are going to inspect some hussy from a back-slum.''

Emma herself was nearly ready to abandon the expedition by the time they reached their destination. To her relief, the address she had been given proved to be on the north side of Great Ormond Street. If less elegant, the houses were actually larger than her own on Park Street in Mayfair, and reasonably well-kept. Philip stopped outside Number Forty-eight.

An urchin appeared instantly and offered to hold the horses. Philip strode up the steps and knocked. The door was opened by a neat maidservant in white apron and cap, and the hall behind her appeared clean and tidy.

Emma had not waited for his assistance in descending from the carriage. "It looks like a perfectly respectable residence,'' she said, joining him.

"I shall return for you in precisely half an hour.''

She smiled at him. "I think I shall survive that long.'' She followed the maid into the house.

The room into which she was ushered was old-fashioned and shabby. Emma scarcely noticed the threadbare furnishings as she found herself the cynosure of six pairs of eyes. Her gaze was drawn immediately to a massive woman in an extraordinary garment of buttercup yellow with silver spangles, who was struggling to rise from her chair. From her emanated an exotic oriental perfume.

The tall gentleman standing by the fireplace put his hand out to stay her. "I daresay Lady Emma will excuse your not rising, Mrs. Winkle." He stepped forward. "Allow me to introduce myself, ma'am. I am Ralph Osborne, a colleague of the late Aloysius Winkle." He bowed, and went on to present the rest of the company.

He was very good-looking, with sun-bleached hair and a tanned face, and his deep voice had a calm, almost soothing quality. Emma found herself listening to it instead of heeding his words, until he named Miss Alison Larkin. The girl who curtsied to her with a cheerful, friendly smile was a veritable sprite. She had sparkling blue eyes in a piquant face, a complexion like rose petals, and a mop of black curls that would inspire the best coiffeur. Even the hideous navy-blue gown did not hide her dainty figure.

"How do you do, my lady," she said, and Emma breathed a sigh of relief. There was no hint of vulgarity in her speech.

Mrs. Winkle waited with obvious impatience while the maid brought in tea and a plate of shortbread. Alison poured the tea, simply and neatly, without any pretence of elegance, which was just as well as the pot was earthenware and the cups and saucers of appallingly thick white china. Emma was agreeably surprised when she nibbled on a piece of shortbread and it melted in her mouth.

"Delicious," she murmured graciously. "My compliments to your cook."

To her horror the plump, pink-faced Miss Larkin—Miss Cleo, was it?—grew even pinker.

"Aunt Cleo made the shortbread, ma'am," Alison confirmed her horrid suspicion. "She is a splendid baker."

Perhaps Philip was right and she ought not even to consider taking on the come-out of a girl, however pretty and wealthy, from so unrefined a background.

Emma was afraid her doubt must have showed in her face, for Mrs. Winkle made an expansive gesture and said firmly, "I only returned from India a week since, my lady. I've not had time yet to make everything pukka. You'll know how to teach Alison to go on properly in Society. I daresay she'll learn quickly, for after all, blood tells, they say, and her grandfather was a viscount."

Alison gasped. A viscount! Her aunts had never told her much about her dead parents and she had always assumed that her mother came from the same solid merchant background as her father. However, the elegant, dignified lady who was to be her chaperon appeared unsurprised and a trifle wary.

"A viscount?" she enquired.

"Yes, indeed, and all on the right side of the blanket, my lady, so you needn't think otherwise. Alison's mama was daughter to Lord Deverill of Ballycarrick, for all he cast her off without a penny when she married our brother."

"Ah, I see. An Irish title."

Alison's euphoria faded. "Is an Irish title not...not a genuine title?" she asked humbly.

Lady Emma's smile was kind. "Perfectly genuine, my dear."

"Then please, ma'am, will you let me come and live with you, and show me how to go on?"

"Why, if your aunt is satisfied . . . ?"

Alison looked anxiously at Aunt Zenobia, who beamed her approval.

"I'd say you're a pukka mem-sahib, my lady, who'll do right by our girl. And you needn't think I'll be poking my nose in where I'm not wanted. There's just the rupees and annas to be settled then. Off with you now, Alison, for it's not proper for young girls to bother their heads with money matters. You won't mind, my lady, if Mr. Osborne stays? He's by way of being my business wallah since poor Winkle popped off."

The three unmarried aunts took the hint and trailed out after Alison.

"You do like Lady Emma, don't you, dear?" asked Aunt Di. "We wouldn't want you to go if you feel the least bit uncomfortable, whatever Zenobia may say."

"Even as a girl, Zenobia was apt to ride roughshod over anyone in her way," Aunt Cleo grunted. She was not at all happy with the turmeric and coriander and fenugreek her sister had pressed upon her with instructions in their use.

Aunt Polly nodded agreement.

Alison flew from one to the next with reassuring hugs and kisses. "Oh, yes, I like Lady Emma. She is so very graceful and refined and composed, I am sure I cannot do better than to try to be like her. And when she smiled, her eyes smiled, too."

Satisfied, the aunts went about their business. Alison lingered in the hall. The talk of rupees and annas seemed interminable. She was beginning to fear that some disagreement had arisen which might spoil the whole affair, when there was a peremptory rapping at the front door.

She started towards it, failing to remember that the household now boasted a maid, one of whose duties was to answer the door. At that moment three balls of white fur raced into view from the back of the house, yipping their joy at seeing her. Midnight followed at a more staid pace.

Bess, the new maid, must have gone out into the garden, forgetting that the dogs were supposed to be shut out of the house while Lady Emma was there. Alison was in a quandary. The terriers must be chased out, but the door knocker was sounding again, plied with a vigorous urgency that brooked no denial.

"Sit, Drop," she ordered. "Sit, Flake and Goose." She opened the door.

The gentleman on the doorstep looked her up and down with an air of cool appraisal. He was of middle height, elegantly if quietly dressed, with no more than two modest capes to his greatcoat. His features were clear-cut but nothing out of the ordinary except, perhaps, his determined chin. Alison took instant exception to the faint boredom in his brown eyes.

"I have come to fetch Lady Emma," he announced. "My name is Trevelyan. Be so good as to announce me to your mistress, girl."

"I am Alison Larkin," she corrected him.

The terriers decided hopefully that she was giving them permission to move. They scampered to greet the stranger, two of them sniffing suspiciously at the ankles of his gleaming top-boots while Flake, the boldest, jumped up to place two paws on his knee and look him in the face.

"Down!" said Alison and Mr. Trevelyan with one voice.

Flake obeyed instantly, leaving two muddy paw prints on the hitherto immaculate dove-coloured inexpressibles. A flush of annoyance stained the high cheekbones, which lent the gentleman's face a sensitivity at odds with his manner.

Alison succeeded in smothering a giggle, but before she could apologize, Midnight sauntered up. Mr. Trevelyan stood his ground.

"I trust your Newfoundland has better manners," he said grimly.

"Oh, yes." She favoured him with a sunny smile. Anyone who recognized the breed could not be all bad. "If Midnight was in the habit of doing that, people would go over like ninepins. The terriers are very intelligent too, but quite irrepressible. Won't you come in, sir? I daresay Lady Emma will be ready to leave shortly."

"I trust she is ready now, Miss Larkin, for I will not leave my cattle standing in this chill."

"Who is holding them?" Alison glanced into the street. "What a splendid rig. Is it a tilbury? And I do think chestnut horses are quite the prettiest. Oh, that's Bubble at their heads. You can trust him with them. Bubble!" she called, "walk the horses for the gentleman."

"Ri'chare, miss." The boy grinned, gap-toothed.

She noticed that Mr. Trevelyan was staring at her in astonishment. Doubtless it was less than decorous behaviour to shout to ragamuffins in the street, but she was only trying to make sure his horses were well cared for. He need not look so disapproving.

She repeated her invitation, with less enthusiasm, and he stepped into the house, doffing his glossy beaver. It seemed to Alison that his very presence made the hallway shabbier than ever.

"I shall inform Lady Emma that you have arrived, Mr. Trevelyan," she said with what she hoped was dignified formality. Then a horrid thought struck her. "You are not a lord, are you? You did not say."

"No, Miss Larkin, I am not a lord."

"Good." She breathed a sigh of relief as she slipped into the parlour—the drawing-room, as Aunt Zenobia insisted on calling it—careful to shut the dogs out. What a great pity it would be if the first lord she ever met proved to be so odiously toplofty.

"Pray excuse me, Aunt Zenobia. A gentleman has called for Lady Emma."

"Philip here already?" The silver-grey ostrich plumes on Lady Emma's charcoal velvet hat bobbed as she stood up. "We are agreed then, Mrs. Winkle. Your lawyer will draw up the papers and Alison shall come to me on Monday. Thank you for your assistance, Mr. Osborne."

Ralph Osborne had also risen to his feet, and now he bowed over her ladyship's hand with a polished politeness that surprised Alison. He had visited several times in the past week without showing the slightest sign of a penchant for gallantry, which was scarce surprising at his age, of course. She was beginning to think of him as an honorary uncle.

As soon as Lady Emma, Mr. Trevelyan and Mr. Osborne had departed, Aunt Zenobia summoned

Alison into the drawing-room to explain the arrangements that had been made for her Season.

"Her ladyship's a sensible young woman," she informed her niece, "for all she's daughter to an earl and widow of a baron. She'll see you have a bit of fun without coming to grief. Mrs. Colonel Bowditch has never steered me wrong yet."

Alison kept to herself her opinion as to who did the steering in that relationship. "I am to go to Lady Emma's on Monday?" she asked.

"The sooner the better, for the Season's none so far off and there's gowns to be bought and all sorts of fallals. All the bills will be sent to me, my dear, for I don't want you troubled with such things. I can stand the nonsense, so you needn't worry your pretty head. And you'll have two pounds a week in your pocket for pin-money."

"Two pounds! I'm sure I could not spend half so much, Aunt."

"I doubt you'll find any difficulty there. You are not to be skimping and saving, mind. You'll be getting all I have one of these days, and you'll be a wealthy woman after I'm gone."

"Oh, Aunt!"

"In the meantime, as I've told Lady Emma, I've set aside something for a dowry. Now I don't want you thinking you have to find yourself a husband in a hurry. There's always Ralph."

"Mr. Osborne?"

"Why, yes. Didn't I tell you he's come home to find himself a bride and settle in England, and he'd be glad to make a match of it with my little niece?"

"With me? But he is quite middle-aged!"

"Nonsense, child, he has no more than five or six and thirty years in his dish. I don't mean to push at you but he's a pukka sahib and a rich man, and kind-hearted to boot. You'll do well to consider his offer, for you could do a deal worse."

"I'm sure it is very obliging of Mr. Osborne to want to marry me, but he is not even a Sir or an Honourable. Indeed, Aunt, I think I should prefer to marry a lord."

"A lord! Here's high flying, if you like. I tell you straight, you'll do better to stick to your own kind, my dear. Much good it ever did your poor papa taking a wife above his station. Bless your heart, you've been addling your noddle with too many novels, I make no doubt," she said indulgently. "Well, I shan't stand in your way, but I daresay a couple of months cavorting with the hote tong will make you appreciate a fine, honest fellow like Ralph Osborne."

Try as she might, Alison could not reconcile Mr. Osborne with her image of a romantic hero. Though admittedly quite good-looking for his advanced age, he lacked both the fiery passion and the delicate sensibilities necessary to a rescuer of damsels in distress. She was a reasonable girl. As she was by no stretch of the imagination in distress she might have settled for one or the other requisite had he possessed a title. Alas, he was not even a member of the untitled aristocracy.

Her thoughts turned to Mr. Philip Trevelyan. Both his friendship with Lady Emma and the haughty disdain of his demeanour proclaimed him a gentleman of the ton—the "hote tong," as Aunt Zenobia would say. It was a pity that he was both disagreeable and dull.

ALISON'S OPINION OF Mr. Trevelyan might have sunk still lower had she been privileged to listen to the conversation as he drove Lady Emma to her home.

"Surely you do not mean to go through with the business," he expostulated.

"Yes, I found her charming, modest and sweet-tempered. Of course her manners need polishing, but I expected that. She has a splendid portion, and is the nabob's widow's heir besides. And if I do not miss my guess, a little judicious pruning will turn her into quite a beauty, and not in the usual style."

"Not in the usual style indeed! I grant you she's a pretty enough child, but it will take more than a little polishing and pruning to render her acceptable, whatever her wealth."

"She has another string to her bow, though I do not mean to make use of it unless it proves necessary. Her mother was Lord Deverill's daughter. Apparently he cast her off when she married a Cit."

"An Irish connexion—doubtless that explains why she put me in mind of a mischievous leprechaun."

"Be charitable, Philip! Elfin is the word that sprang to my mind."

"You did not see her shouting to an urchin in the street, like the veriest hoyden. What is worse, she appeared to be on familiar terms with the brat. 'Bubble,' I believe, was the name she addressed him by."

"Oh, dear! Still, she seems amazingly eager to learn and I daresay a word in her ear on that subject will suffice," said Lady Emma optimistically.

"She is a vulgar, impertinent chit. I fear you will regret this."

They dropped the subject, but Philip failed in his attempt to dismiss Miss Larkin from his mind. He had distinctly heard the girl mutter "good" when he told her he had no title. What the devil had she meant by that?

CHAPTER THREE

"I LOOK JUST LIKE MAMA." Alison gazed entranced at the vision in the gilt-framed mirror on Lady Emma's dressing-table. The unruly mop of black was gone, and in its place a cluster of soft, glossy curls framed her face. "Thank you, Miss Carter, you have cut it splendidly. If you will tell me where to find a dustpan and brush I shall clear up this mess."

Though seeming pleased by the compliment, the abigail raised her eyebrows in surprise. "That won't be necessary, miss. The chambermaid will see to it in a trice."

"Let us go to your chamber and decide what you are to wear today," said Lady Emma hurriedly.

"Oh yes, ma'am." Alison's smile revealed a dimple hitherto hidden by her locks. "All my new gowns are so pretty, I vow it will take an age to choose."

Though small, Alison's chamber was a delightful place, decorated with frivolous frills and ruffles of primrose-and-white muslin. A coal fire glowed in the grate, before which there was just room for a pair of elegant rosewood armchairs upholstered in pale yellow brocade. Lady Emma motioned Alison to one of these and sat down in the other. She leaned forward with an earnest expression.

"My dear, you must not be offering to do the servants' work for them. It is not at all the thing."

"I beg your pardon. I am not used to having servants, you see, except for Mrs. 'Arris—Harris—three days a week, though Aunt Zenobia hired a maid and Mrs. Colonel Bowditch is helping her find more. Besides, Miss Carter cut my hair so beautifully, it did not seem fair that she should have to sweep up the debris as well."

"And do not call her *Miss* Carter, pray."

"Is she married? I hope I have not offended her."

Lady Emma sighed. "No, I am sure you have not, but it is proper for you to call her simply Carter."

"I am shockingly ignorant, am I not? Pray do not despair, I *will* learn."

"Of course you will. Now, let us see which dress you are to put on."

Alison opened her wardrobe. Its sparse contents seemed to her like riches. There were two morning gowns, one of white muslin sprigged with pink rosebuds and the other white cambric embellished with knots of green ribbon at the high waist and down the front of the skirt. Beside them hung a pale blue walking dress and a dark blue pelisse. Lady Emma's dressmaker had run them up in a hurry and was working on several more, though Alison could not imagine when she would wear so many.

"The sprig muslin will do. I am expecting one or two callers this afternoon."

"This afternoon? Shall I dust the... No, I daresay your parlourmaid has already dusted the drawing-room. I wish there was something I could do for you," said Alison wistfully. "You are so very kind to me. Would it be all right if I made you a cap? I always made my aunts', but they are very plain. I should enjoy working with satin ribbons and lace."

"Nothing could be better. Needlework is an eminently suitable occupation for young ladies, and I am always glad of a pretty new cap. Carter shall find you a piece of muslin and some odds and ends of ribbon so that you will have something to occupy your hands this afternoon."

"Is Mr. Trevelyan coming? He is a good friend of yours, I think."

"I do not particularly expect him, but he may call. I have known Philip since I was a child. He was used to pull my pigtails."

"I cannot imagine him being a naughty boy." She was astonished. "He seemed prodigious starchy and proper and I fear he disapproves of me."

"Philip's opinion need not concern us. Mrs. Talmadge's is another matter. She will be one of our guests this afternoon. I want you to sit quite quietly and listen to the conversation. Of course you will answer when spoken to, but she rarely pauses to allow anyone else a word. That is why I invited her to drink tea today."

Alison laughed. At first she had been nonplussed by her chaperon's dry humour but she was growing accustomed to it. Lady Emma was near to perfection in her eyes, a patterncard to be copied as closely as possible.

Lady Emma wore her dark blond hair plaited and pinned up, with only a few short curls showing beneath her cap, but Alison knew her own hair would never behave so demurely. It was better short. Nor could she remedy her lack of inches, for Lady Emma was somewhat above middle height. However, Alison was determined to strive to emulate the graceful dignity of her mentor's carriage, her composure and serene assurance.

It was difficult, when life was so exciting she felt as if she were full of bubbles and might float away across the rooftops at any moment.

The drawing-room had indeed been dusted by the competent parlourmaid. Nonetheless, Alison found herself looking automatically for dog hairs on the red-and-cream striped satin sofas. Naturally there were none, nor dog nose smears on the window panes. The satinwood tables gleamed, the Axminster carpet was spotless, the whole room breathed a calm, cheerful elegance.

Into this haven trotted Mrs. Talmadge. She was a tall, thin woman, dressed in Pomona green with quantities of fluttering scarves draped about her. Her large, unnaturally white teeth presented no obstacle to the endless stream of words that flowed from her lips.

While Alison's deft fingers fashioned a ruff of tiny pleats and a rosette of buttercup-yellow ribbon, she listened, fascinated, to the gossip. She could not help wondering when the lady ever stopped talking long enough to gather the tidbits she so generously passed on.

"Well, my dear Lady Emma," said Mrs. Talmadge at last, rising to take her leave, "such a comfortable cose as we have had. Good day, Miss Larkin."

Alison hastily set aside her sewing and curtsied. "Good day, ma'am."

"A pretty-behaved child," the visitor said to Lady Emma in a loud whisper, nodding her approval. "She will do."

The footman showed Mrs. Talmadge out. Alison turned to Lady Emma.

"Must I learn to talk so?" she asked.

"By no means. It is not a style of conversation I care for and in a young girl can only give disgust. Henrietta is at least well intentioned."

"How ever does she find out all that information?"

Lady Emma smiled. "I have heard that she employs a maid solely to gather rumors. However, her information is usually accurate and she never invents malicious on-dits, unlike some I could name. She is no scandalmonger—you will have noted that she generally has a kind word to say of everyone. For the next few days she will go about telling all and sundry that my latest protégée is a pretty-behaved girl."

Alison clapped her hands. "How clever you are!"

"I must return the compliment. What a charming confection you have created from a few bits and pieces."

"Do you like it? Caps are quite easy. I once tried to stitch up a gown and I made a sad mull of it. Aunt Di had to take the whole thing apart and start again from the beginning."

"Well, there is no need for you to be sewing your own gowns, but I think it a very good plan for you always to have some fine work about you. Needlework is a ladylike occupation and provides an unexceptionable topic of conversation. Besides, if you are not sure what to say, you can always set a few stitches while you are considering. I shall give you my tapestry work-bag. It is pretty enough to carry about with you."

Her advice proved useful a few minutes later, when another caller arrived. The Honourable Robert Gilchrist, Lady Emma's younger brother, was a gentleman of poetical aspirations. His stocky form was clad in a crimson velvet coat with an embroidered silk waistcoat and a multicoloured silk handkerchief about his neck in place of a cravat.

His flowery compliments put Alison to the blush, and she was glad to be able to bow her head over her needle.

"He said my eyes made him think of woodlands full of bluebells," she told Lady Emma later.

"Highly unoriginal," said his unimpressed sister. "Robert is quite harmless, however. You need not take anything he says seriously, which is fortunate as it is impossible to take seriously anything said by anyone dressed in that extraordinary manner."

"I did think his clothes a little unusual," Alison confessed.

"He thinks they make him look like a poet. I fear he was deeply impressed by a portrait of Lord Byron in Turkish dress, though he does not go quite so far, thank heaven. He can usually be persuaded to dress conventionally for an evening party, and as he is an excellent dancer he will do as an escort until you are acquainted with a few gentlemen. The dancing master comes tomorrow for your first lesson. I must give orders to have the carpet in the drawing-room rolled back."

Learning to dance was not the unalloyed pleasure Alison had expected. Signor Pascoli was tall and thin, with a drooping moustache. According to Lady Emma, his air of romantic melancholy made him the most fashionable dancing master in London. Whenever Alison turned left instead of right or curtsied when she should have promenaded, he sighed as if his heart was breaking, his dark, liquid eyes reproachful.

"And he hums out of tune!" she said indignantly.

"I shall play the spinet for your next lesson."

"It seems odd to be learning English country dances like the Lancers and the Dashing White Sergeant from an Italian."

"He is a good teacher. You are picking up the steps remarkably quickly. Of course, that is partly because you are an excellent pupil."

"Because the faster I learn, the fewer lessons I shall have to take from him!"

"I daresay, but in general I am excessively pleased with the way you remember my suggestions. You never repeat a mistake."

"I am trying very hard. I cannot expect a lord to fall in love with me if I do not behave like a lady."

"A lord to fall in love with you? You are looking to break a few hearts, are you?" asked Lady Emma, smiling.

"Oh, no, I would not want to hurt anyone's feelings. When he falls at my feet and offers his heart I shall not refuse him. Would it not be the most romantic thing in the world?"

A look of pensive sadness crossed Lady Emma's face. It was a moment before she spoke, and then there was a hint of irony in her gentle tone. "Vastly romantic. Have you a particular lord in mind?"

"I am not acquainted with any. I shall meet some, shall I not?"

"That much I can guarantee. I hope you are not expecting too much of your Season, Alison. I doubt, for instance, whether it is worth applying for vouchers to Almack's." She frowned in thought. "Though it might be managed, I vow. Philip is on excellent terms with Castlereagh, and Lady Castlereagh is one of the patronesses."

"But Mr. Trevelyan does not approve of me," Alison reminded her. "You must not think I mind not attending Almack's. I know the subscription balls are monstrous exclusive, but my friend Letty told me she heard that the rooms are nothing out of the ordinary and the suppers are positively nipcheese. Is it true they serve only lemonade and bread and butter?"

"And stale cake."

"Then I do not care if I never go. After all, I never expected any of this at all." Her gesture embraced the world of high society, of balls and fine clothes and elegant surroundings. "I thought I should have to choose between dwindling into an old maid like my aunts or marrying the apothecary's assistant, who has damp hands and a drip on the end of his nose. Sometimes I think I shall wake up in the morning and find that everything has vanished, like Cinders's magic coach. So I mean to enjoy every minute, then I shall have pleasant memories of dancing with lords even if I never find one who wishes to marry me."

"I shall see that you have those memories," Lady Emma promised. "But forgive me, your aunt gave me to understand that you are as good as betrothed to Mr. Osborne."

"I am not! Can you think of anything less romantic than a middle-aged India merchant? Aunt Zenobia said only that if I do not find a husband this spring, Mr. Osborne is willing to take me as his bride."

"I see. Then you are perfectly free to have any number of peers swooning at your feet."

"Have you read Mrs. Cuthbertson's novels?" asked Alison eagerly. "Letty has lent me most of them. I do think, though, that her heroes and heroines waste a lot of time in fainting fits. We counted them in one book,

Santo Sebastiano I think it was, and there were twenty-seven swoons altogether. I have never fainted in my life. Perhaps you could teach me how?''

Lady Emma laughed. "If you are going to swoon, I daresay you ought to know how to do so gracefully. I have never fainted myself, you understand, but the most important point, I believe, is to be sure that the correct gentleman is standing in the right position to catch you.''

"And I expect one ought to give him some sort of warning," said Alison with a giggle. "It would be horridly disconcerting to hit the ground before he realized what was happening!''

"Horrid! Heavens, look at the time. We have shopping to do today. Run and change into your walking dress."

The door knocker sounded as Alison was crossing the hall. She managed to resist a momentary feeling that she ought to answer the summons, and she was half-way up the stairs when the footman, Henry, opened the door. Curious, she paused.

"Is Lady Emma at home?" enquired Mr. Trevelyan's languid voice.

Alison had not the least desire to meet him again. She went on up to her chamber, frowning. It was ridiculous to allow the man to intimidate her, but there was no point pretending he did not make her feel uncomfortable. She was not used to being looked upon with disfavour, for in general she liked people and they returned the compliment. What a pity that he was such a good friend of Lady Emma's. She was bound to see a good deal of him.

Common sense came to the rescue. She had no way of changing his opinion, and as long as he did not turn

Lady Emma against her, whether he liked her or not made no difference to her. She would ignore his disapprobation and treat him as she would anyone else.

As she took the blue walking dress from the wardrobe, she could not help hoping that the odious Mr. Trevelyan would at least notice the improvement in her appearance.

CHAPTER FOUR

MR. TREVELYAN HAD NOTICED a neat ankle disappear round the turn of the stairs as he stepped into Lady Emma's front hall. He averted his eyes. He had never denied Miss Larkin's physical attractions, he told himself. It was her upbringing he objected to.

"So the girl has moved in," he greeted his friend. "I hoped you had changed your mind."

"On the contrary, I am growing quite fond of Alison already. She is quick to learn, and excessively grateful for instruction. She made the cap I am wearing."

"Vastly becoming, but that does not alter my opinion of the chit. She is not setting up as a milliner, after all—though come to think of it that might be the very thing for her. You are inviting trouble, trying to persuade the Polite World to accept her."

"Take care, Philip. You are beginning to sound like a cross-grained old bachelor twice your age. I own that with her background I cannot expect her to take the ton by storm, but I do not doubt that she will have a modest success. Nor do I despair of her reaching her goal. She has set her heart on marrying a lord."

"She told you so? At least she has the merit of honesty, the mercenary, vulgar little wretch."

"Hardly mercenary," said Emma drily, "when her aunt's fortune is enough to buy and sell a dozen peers I could name."

Philip was taken aback, but he quickly rallied. "So she merely wants to purchase a title. It is not uncommon these days, to be sure, but no less distasteful for that."

"You only think so because the Trevelyans have steadfastly rejected a peerage these past five hundred years. *My* ancestor was happy to provide Henry VII with funds in exchange for his earldom. How determined you are to think ill of Alison! She is still unused to her sudden prosperity and I do not believe the notion of purchasing a title ever crossed her mind. Far from being a 'vulgar wretch,' she is simply a romantic child."

"I suppose you will tell me next that she is a slave to Minerva Press novels?"

"But of course."

"I might have guessed."

"As I was at that age," she observed.

He laughed and capitulated. "Very well, you win. I suppose you want me to help you to establish her."

"Will you, Philip? I confess I should be glad of your support, since she has no connexions of her own to assist us. Robert has agreed to escort us, but he is such a mooncalf that that will impress no one. I believe he is in the throes of a sonnet to her eyes."

"He will grow out of it. You must admit poetry is preferable to the days when he was forever challenging all and sundry to duels."

"Yes, but what will he fall into next? Ah, Alison, come and make your curtsy to Mr. Trevelyan."

Philip turned. A curious sensation in his chest robbed him of breath as he took in the enchanting vision poised in the doorway. From the artless froth of ebony curls to the tips of her blue kid half-boots, Miss Alison Larkin was a delight to the eye.

She advanced into the room with a tread so light he thought again of leprechauns. The mischievous twinkle in her eyes was missing, however. Their vivid blue was no less brilliant than he remembered, but they seemed larger, more expressive, and there was a hint of wariness in their depths. Her smile was friendly, though, and her curtsy a model of decorum. He wondered why he was trying so hard to dislike her.

And why, if she wanted to marry a lord, had she been so pleased to discover that he was not one?

"Will you allow me the pleasure of driving you in Hyde Park this afternoon, Miss Larkin?" he enquired. It would be a feather in her cap to be seen taking the air in his carriage, for he rarely took up females.

"Thank you, sir, but I believe Lady Emma has other plans." She was unperturbed.

Ridiculously disappointed, he glanced at Emma. She appeared amused.

"We really must do some shopping today, Philip. Tomorrow, perhaps, if it is fine?"

"I must be at the House at four tomorrow, but we might go to the Park early. Will two o'clock do?"

Emma nodded.

"That will be delightful," said Miss Larkin primly.

She did not sound delighted, nor did she appear to be aware of the signal honour he was granting her. He took his leave in something of a miff.

The door had scarcely closed behind him when Lady Emma said, "I do hope Mrs. Gribbins has finished your carriage dress. We shall go to her first."

"But I can wear this gown," Alison protested. "I know you called it a walking dress, but it will be perfectly comfortable in a carriage, too."

"Possibly, but Philip saw you in that one today. It will never do to wear the same again tomorrow. Come and put on your bonnet, we must be off."

Alison followed her from the room. "You mean I cannot wear this dress again? But it is so pretty, and I have the matching pelisse and bonnet." Dismayed, she looked down at the pale blue jaconet with its ruffles of white mull muslin. The bonnet, which she had set on the hall table when she came downstairs, had blue silk roses about the crown; she could not bear the thought of wearing such a delightful confection only once.

Lady Emma reassured her. "Certainly you shall wear the outfit again, but not for a few days, not when you expect to see Philip."

"I cannot believe he would notice what I am wearing, still less remember what I wore the day before, nor care if he did!"

"You are probably right, you sceptical child. It is chiefly for other females that we dress to the nines. We need not rush off to Mrs. Gribbins then."

"Oh yes, let us go there first. After all, Mr. Trevelyan *might* notice." Alison laughed at herself. "Perhaps it is really for our own satisfaction that we put on fine feathers."

For her own satisfaction, then, Alison was glad to find that the mantua-maker had indeed finished her slate-grey carriage dress with the coquelicot ribbons, and another three morning gowns besides.

And it was purely for her own satisfaction that she spent an hour preparing for her drive in the Park the next day. So she told herself, at least, as she tried to decide whether the new velvet bonnet with the curly ostrich feather or the straw hat with its bunch of cherries best complemented the carriage dress. Her attire must be perfect—well, perhaps not solely for her own satisfaction, she admitted, but to boost her self-confidence. Mr. Trevelyan must have thawed somewhat towards her to issue the invitation, but he still made her feel a trifle uneasy.

She decided the bonnet was more dignified.

When he came to fetch her, his demeanour did nothing to set her up in her own esteem. He handed her into the smart, moss-green tilbury with such an air of insufferable boredom that she nearly insisted on descending again at once.

She refused to be intimidated. As he set his chestnuts in motion, she settled back in the comfortable seat and ventured to ask the horses' names.

"Spaniard and Conqueror."

"Something to do with the Duke of Wellington?" she hazarded a guess. "No, I have it! How very clever." She went off into peals of laughter.

Mr. Trevelyan glanced at her in astonishment, then grinned. He looked almost boyish. "Never say you have worked it out. You are one in a thousand, Miss Larkin."

"It's because they are chestnuts, is it not? The sweet chestnut is called a Spanish chestnut, hence Spaniard, and the boys' name for the horse chestnut is conker, which you have expanded to Conqueror. Bubble and Squeak play endless games with conkers tied to bits of string."

"You try to smash your opponent's conker. I was something of a champion in my youth. Bubble—was that not the name of the urchin who walked my cattle in Great Ormond Street?''

"Yes, and Squeak is his brother. Those are not their real names, of course. The two of them and Tarry Joe are the regulars of Aunt Cleo's gang; the others come and go." She hesitated. "I think Lady Emma would say that I ought not to have mentioned them."

"You are quite right, but permit me to ask, what exactly is Aunt Cleo's gang?" Mr. Trevelyan was no longer the light-hearted gentleman who had played conkers in his youth. He looked positively grim.

Obviously Lady Emma was justified in forbidding talk of the boys. "No, I must not talk about them," Alison said firmly. "What delightful weather we are having."

The sun was shining and the gentle breeze carried a balmy promise of spring. The tilbury passed the Grosvenor Gate and entered Hyde Park, where a number of carriages and horsemen were already taking advantage of the fine day. Alison saw that early daffodils were trumpeting under the elms.

Forgetting her companion's relapse into hauteur, she cried out, "Oh look, are they not pretty? Aunt Polly's were scarce budding when I left. Daffodils are my favourite flower—at least until the roses bloom, and I am very fond of chrysanthemums, and lavender of course, for the sweet smell, and—"

"Flowers in general." Mr. Trevelyan's lips twitched. "Do you wish to pick some?" He reined in Spaniard and Conqueror.

"Yes, but I have a lowering feeling that Lady Emma would not approve. Thank you, but I had best not."

He drove on. "You are very determined to do what will please Emma."

"She is so kind to me, I should hate to disappoint her. Tomorrow she will take me to meet her sister, Bella, who is just come up to Town. That is Lady Fairfield, is it not? I am to practice my company manners, for Lady Fairfield is too indolent and good-natured to take exception if I make a mistake."

"Emma takes all her protégées to practice on Bella," he said, laughing. "You will like her. In fact, all the Gilchrists are pleasant people."

"I hardly ever meet anyone I do not like." Alison decided Mr. Trevelyan was quite handsome when he was amused. There was a warm twinkle in the brown eyes she had thought so daunting. "People in general are very agreeable, are they not? Only yesterday, when we were shopping, I made a new friend." She giggled.

"Do you mean to tell me the joke?"

"It is not worth recounting, but I shall not leave you on tenterhooks. I was looking at some bugle trimming when a thread broke and the beads scattered all over the counter. There were dozens, rolling about and dropping on the floor. I had not the least notion what to do! I must have looked at a loss, for the young lady next to me seized the ribbon from me and said in a loud voice, 'Look, Mama, this is very inferior stuff. It has fallen apart in my hand.'"

"Both sympathetic and quick-witted."

"Was she not? I was excessively grateful not to be left standing there like a ninnyhammer. The shopman was full of apologies. He brought out a better quality of trimming and I purchased some, so you need not think that he suffered too badly as a result of my clumsiness."

"I have no doubt the accident was due to inferior quality, as the young lady said, not to your clumsiness. Did you learn her name?"

"That is the best of all: she is Miss Witherington and her mama is Lady Witherington, who is acquainted with Lady Emma. And Lady Emma has asked them to tea next week. Am I not lucky? It was altogether a splendid day."

"You enjoy shopping, I collect."

"I did buy some very pretty things. Have you ever been to Schomberg House in Pall Mall, to Harding and Howell's? They sell everything you can imagine, clocks and parasols and gowns, all in different departments separated by mahogany partitions with windows and glass doors. Upstairs there are even glass domes in the ceiling to let in daylight. It is as grand as a palace! Oh look, I believe the gentleman riding towards us is trying to catch your eye."

Mr. Trevelyan glanced at the rider. "That is Lord Fane. Are you ready to meet your first lord, Miss Larkin, or shall I pretend I have not seen him?" There was a teasing note to his voice.

Alison rose to the challenge. "Pray introduce us, sir," she said somewhat breathlessly, sitting up straighter. A stream of Lady Emma's instructions raced through her head as the tilbury drew to a halt and the gentlemen exchanged greetings.

"Miss Larkin," said Mr. Trevelyan, "allow me to make Lord Fane known to you."

"How do you do, my lord," she murmured, eyes lowered, then risked a glance upward.

His lordship was gazing down at her with a look of bemused admiration in his grey eyes that brought a flush to her cheeks. He had removed his curly-brimmed beaver to bow to her, revealing fair hair cut in a fashionable Brutus. His nose, she was gratified to note, was the superb epitome of aristocratic breeding.

"I am happy to make your acquaintance, Miss Larkin. You are newly come to Town, I daresay?"

He could not have begun with a more difficult question if he had tried, Alison thought indignantly. She had spent all her life in Town, but moving in quite the wrong circles.

"Indeed, my lord," she murmured.

Mr. Trevelyan seemed to be quivering with silent laughter beside her, which made it difficult to concentrate on what Lord Fane was saying. Fortunately, he spoke the merest commonplace courtesies.

"Delightful weather for the time of year, is it not, ma'am?"

"Yes, my lord."

"Alas, we cannot expect that it will continue."

"No, my lord."

"If March comes in like a lamb, it will go out like a lion, they say."

"Yes, my lord."

"I have always considered that there is a great deal of wisdom in such country sayings."

"Yes, my lord."

He continued in this vein and she was able to answer, "Yes, my lord," and "No, my lord," without perjuring herself. At last he asked if he might do himself the honour of calling upon her.

She flung a glance of mute appeal at Mr. Trevelyan.

"Miss Larkin is staying with Lady Emma Grant," he said. "I believe you are acquainted with Lady Emma?"

Lord Fane agreed fervently that he was indeed acquainted with her ladyship, distantly related even. He took his leave and rode on.

"That is all very well," said Alison, twisting in her seat to look after him, "but if he calls I shall have to converse with him properly."

Mr. Trevelyan chuckled. "Emma will preserve you from him until you are ready. However, if I am not mistaken he is the kind that prefers young ladies to be demure and respectfully attentive to what he says. You managed it very well."

"It was not easy with you sitting there trying not to laugh," she accused. "How well he rides! And his coat is excessively elegant. I thought him charming. Does he really know Lady Emma?"

"Emma knows everyone, and besides, the Fanes have some connexion by marriage with the Gilchrists, I believe, as he mentioned. He is several years younger than she, though, so I doubt he knows her well."

"He looked to be five or six and twenty."

"An excellent age," he murmured, so softly she was not sure whether she had heard aright.

His expression was sardonic, but he had been amazingly approachable all afternoon and Alison decided to take advantage of his amiability.

"May I ask you a question, sir?"

"By all means, though of course I cannot promise to answer. And provided I may ask you one next."

She was afraid he was going to ask about the urchins, and that he would poker up again if she told him. "By all means," she said cautiously, "though I cannot promise to answer."

"Touché. Your turn first."

"I have been wondering why Lady Emma does not choose to live with her family, instead of burdening herself with ignorant girls like me. You said the Gilchrists are pleasant people, and she speaks of them with affection. I did not like to ask her, and I expect you will tell me it is none of my business, but surely she would have an easier life if she took up residence with them?"

"Emma does in fact spend much of the year with her family. She was at Fairfield for Christmas with Bella, and last summer she stayed with her parents for several months, but she does not wish to be obliged to live with them. She has a horror of being dependent, so she has kept her own house, and thus retains a certain freedom. She is not so eccentric as to live alone—when she is in London she usually has an elderly cousin with her, who is at present visiting another relative."

"She never speaks of her husband. She must have loved him very much?"

"Miss Larkin, you cannot expect me to answer that! I have already been less than discreet, only because I believe your interest springs from affection."

"It does. I am sorry, I know I ought not to have asked you," she said penitently. "What is your question?"

He hesitated, as if uncertain whether to proceed. "When I came to your house, you asked if I were a lord and I told you I was not. I thought I heard you say 'good,' as you turned away. Why?"

Alison felt absurdly guilty. She did not wish to confess, but it was only fair when he had patiently answered her impertinent query.

"Because I did not like you," she muttered, sure that she was crimson to the roots of her hair. A sideways glance showed her that he, too, was somewhat pink in the face.

"I see. I did not precisely behave so as to ingratiate myself," he said wryly. "May I hope to be forgiven?"

"I like you very well now," she hastened to assure him. "Indeed, I do not know when I have enjoyed anything so much as driving in the Park this afternoon."

"Thank you, Miss Larkin. You mean since yesterday afternoon's shopping expedition, I collect?"

She laughed, glad that he was joking. "I enjoy most things," she admitted.

"I am sorry to bring your enjoyment to an end, but we have been twice about the Park and I must be at the House by four." He directed Conqueror and Spaniard towards the gate. "I hope you will drive out with me again one of these days."

"I should love to, but you must give Lady Emma a turn, too."

Leaving the Park, they drove along Upper Brook Street, then left into Park Street. To her horror, Alison saw Bubble lingering near Lady Emma's front steps. She closed her eyes, sure that Mr. Trevelyan must recognize him.

The tilbury stopped.

"Give me all you have, boy," came Mr. Trevelyan's pleased voice, and suddenly her arms were full of yellow daffodils. "Your favourite flower, I believe, Miss Larkin. At present, at least."

As she raised her eyes to his smiling face, she saw Bubble on the pavement behind him with an empty basket and a delighted, if gap-toothed, grin. He held up a shiny half-sovereign, put his finger to his lips and winked.

CHAPTER FIVE

LADY EMMA'S SISTER, Arabella Fairfield, was a plump, kind-hearted if lazy matron in her mid-thirties. She had two sons at Harrow, and a daughter at school in Bath who would be making her come-out the following year.

"It is positively shocking how they grow up," she observed placidly. "It ages one so. You are prodigious successful at bringing out young girls, Em. I shall rely on you to show me how to go on."

"To do all the hard work, more like," said Lady Emma, shaking her head. "I know you, Bella."

Lady Fairfield chuckled. "All too well, I vow."

Alison liked her. If the other hostesses she would meet in the next few weeks were even half as amiable, her apprehensions were groundless.

When she and Lady Emma returned from the visit, they found that both Mr. Trevelyan and Lord Fane had left cards in their absence. While Lady Emma read the brief message Philip had written on the back of his, Alison picked up his lordship's and gazed at it in awe.

"He really did come to call! Was it not obliging of Mr. Trevelyan to introduce us?"

"Yes, it is more than I expected of him when I asked him to help me establish you. Standing up with you occasionally at a ball was all I had in mind, but I should have known Philip would always make an ex-

tra effort for an old friend. So Lord Fane called! What
do you think of your first lord?''

''To tell the truth I was too overwhelmed to look
properly at his face, except to note that he looks prodigious aristocratic. His riding coat was excessively elegant and he made a fine figure on his horse.''

''And what of his manner?''

''He was all that is civil, even though I did not know
what to say to him. I am glad we were from home when
he called.''

''Hey-day, Alison bashful? It will not last, I vow. I
was exceptionally pleased with the way you spoke with
Bella, and you will soon be ready to face Lord Fane. I
think I shall invite Philip and Robert to a little formal
dinner party to give you some experience at conversation and the etiquette of that sort of occasion.''

''I must quickly read some poetry then, so that I can
converse sensibly with Mr. Gilchrist.''

''I suspect you will find that Robert is interested only
in his own verse, and all you will need to do is admire
it,'' said that young gentleman's sister drily. ''Do you
want to keep Lord Fane's card as a remembrance of
your first meeting with a lord?''

''Oh yes, thank you. I shall put it under my pillow,
and perhaps I shall dream of him.''

Lady Emma shook her head indulgently, and they
went upstairs to put off their bonnets and pelisses. As
they reached the landing, Alison laughed.

''I was just thinking,'' she explained, ''how glad I
am that Lord Fane did not swoon at my feet. As he was
on horseback, he might have done himself a serious
injury!''

She set his lordship's card on her dressing table and
when, a few minutes later, she sat down to tidy her hair,

she picked it up again. It was to Mr. Trevelyan, however, that her thoughts turned.

She should have known that he was only behaving so charmingly towards her for Lady Emma's sake—an extra effort for an old friend. Still, it was a bit disappointing when she had imagined that he might be coming to like her for herself, despite their unfortunate start. Not that his opinion of her really mattered, since he had no title, but she would not give him any cause to refuse to help. Lady Emma would need all the assistance she could find to establish a girl from so obscure a background.

Her eyes focused once more on the card in her hand. Lord Fane seemed to admire her. With a little encouragement he might be persuaded to fall madly in love with her and to propose marriage. It would be excessively romantic to wed the first lord she had ever met.

Mr. Trevelyan had said that Lord Fane preferred demure young ladies. Alison vowed to do her best to become demure.

As she stood up and turned to put the card under her pillow, she saw the huge bowl of daffodils Carter had arranged on her chest of drawers. She smiled. Perhaps Mr. Trevelyan did like her a little, after all.

THIS COMFORTING reflection had to be revised when the gentleman in question called the next day. Alison was performing the complex figures of the quadrille under Signor Pascoli's mournful gaze. It was not easy dancing with an imaginary partner and three other imaginary couples, even when she had invented names and faces for them. With Mr. Trevelyan standing by the spinet talking to Lady Emma, whose timing grew erratic as a consequence, the task became still more difficult. Alison struggled on, thankful when she reached the final curtsy.

Signor Pascoli departed. Alison would have liked to tell Mr. Trevelyan about her pretended fellow dancers, but somehow in Lady Emma's presence it was difficult to recapture the informality of yesterday's conversation. Besides, he was wearing his bored expression.

Lady Emma, however, was cheerful. "You have the steps very well, Alison. I believe one more lesson will be enough. But though Signor Pascoli is excellent for the set dances, it is impossible to learn to waltz properly without a partner. You need to practice with a gentleman."

"Do I sense a cue?" enquired Mr. Trevelyan, at his most sardonic. He performed an elaborate bow to Alison. "I plainly see where my duty lies. Pray grant me the honour of this dance, Miss Larkin."

She accepted graciously, winning a nod of approval from Lady Emma, who began to play. Signor Pascoli had instructed Alison without so much as touching her arm, and at first she was disconcerted to feel Mr. Trevelyan's hand at her waist. However, his expression was so distant that she soon forgot her embarrassment.

If his manner was stiff, his dancing was far from it. He spun her about the room until she felt she was flying. It was a sad let-down when the music stopped and she sank in a breathless curtsy.

"Really, Philip, did you have to make the child giddy?" Lady Emma reproved, laughing.

"No effort on my part was necessary," he said enigmatically. "She followed my lead beautifully. May I hope you will stand up with me at Almack's, Miss Larkin?''

"Thank you, sir, I should love to but I do not expect to attend the assemblies there."

He raised his eyebrows. "You don't sound devastated. Perhaps you have not heard Henry Luttrell's verse:

"All on that magic LIST depends,
Fame, fortune, fashion, lovers, friends:
'Tis that which gratifies or vexes
All ranks, all ages, and both sexes.
If once to Almack's you belong,
Like monarchs, you can do no wrong;
But banished thence on Wednesday night,
By Jove, you can do nothing right."

Lady Emma frowned. Alison thought it unkind of him to point out to her the disadvantages of her situation, but she would not allow him the satisfaction of knowing she minded.

She said tranquilly, "Indeed, I am having so much fun already, I cannot think that I shall miss that one experience. Lady Emma says I shall be going to any number of parties and balls. And I understand the suppers at Almack's consist of bread and butter and stale cake! I am used to better fare, I promise you, for my aunt Cleo is a splendid cook."

This time Lady Emma's frown was directed at her. "My dear, I beg you will not be forever talking about your aunts."

"No, ma'am, I shall try not to, but you must not expect me to disown them." She felt her cheeks grow hot with indignation.

"Of course not," said Mr. Trevelyan calmly. "You have not seen your family, I think, since you came here. Perhaps you would permit me to take you to visit them one day?"

Surprised and grateful, she accepted. She did not know what to make of him. One moment he implied that she was a giddy girl and prophesied dire consequences of her inability to obtain vouchers for Almack's. The next, he defended her against Lady Emma and offered to take her to a house he had clearly despised on sight. There was no understanding the man.

Had she but known it, Philip did not understand himself. He had always prided himself on his level-headed common sense, the superiority of his taste and the regularity of his habits. His work absorbed his energies, though he did not neglect his social life. If there was anything he detested it was vulgarity, yet here he was, lending countenance to the foisting on the ton of a chit with no pretensions to gentility.

He admired Alison's determination not to cast off her plebeian aunts. That scarcely seemed reason enough for him to drive her to that appalling neighbourhood to see them!

Only his sense of duty kept him from crying off. Though he had made the offer on the spur of the moment, he realized that the visit would serve his purpose very well. He had resolved to investigate "Aunt Cleo's gang," but it made him uncomfortable to have an ulterior motive for what Miss Larkin doubtless saw as an act of kindness. Either she was the innocent she appeared, or else she was a superb actress. He hated the thought that she might be mixed up in anything havey-cavey.

ON THE DAY OF THE OUTING, the chill drizzle that fell
unrelentingly all morning dealt a death blow to his enthusiasm, never robust. Stoically he set off for Emma's house, hoping that her protégée would have the
wit to choose to stay home in such inclement weather.

"But surely your carriage has a hood?" she asked in
surprise when he suggested a postponement. "And an
apron?"

"Yes, and I have brought an umbrella," he admitted grudgingly.

"Then I do not see why... Oh, I beg your pardon,
perhaps it is inconvenient for you to take me?"

"Not at all." He was unable to bring himself to disappoint her. "Let us be off."

It was impossible to remain disgruntled with a pretty
young lady—he would provisionally grant her that
status—sitting beside him and commenting with pleasure on the most unlikely things.

"How green the grass is in the rain," she said as they
crossed the top of Grosvenor Square. "The trees must
be drinking, and preparing themselves to burst into
leaf. Spring is quite the nicest season of the year."

"Until summer comes?" he teased. "Autumn has its
pleasures, too, and even winter. A crisp, clear day with
the world blanketed with snow is as beautiful as any
sight I know, and nothing can beat coming in out of the
cold and roasting chestnuts by a roaring fire."

"I have never seen clean snow," she said wistfully.
"In London it is grey before it touches the ground."

Nor was she accustomed to a roaring fire, he realized. A poverty-stricken winter in Town must indeed
make spring a welcome arrival. "Are you cold?" he
asked.

"Not at all. I have my new muff. I had thought to buy fur, but Lady Emma said it is ostentatious and I am sure it could not be warmer than mine. This is stuffed with feathers, you see, and the cover matches my cloak. Is it not splendid? I hope your hands are not cold? I would lend you my muff but I cannot quite see how you would drive."

"I shall pass the reins to you, of course."

She laughed. She had the most delightful laugh, full of gaiety with a hint of mischief, matching the twinkle of her blue eyes. "I think even two such well-behaved horses as Spaniard and Conqueror might take exception to that," she teased in return, "but I am willing to try, if you wish to borrow the muff."

"Heaven forbid. The art of driving a pair is not mastered in a few minutes, Miss Larkin."

"I rather thought not. Oh, do not turn here. If you go round the other way the streets are much pleasanter."

Philip was not used to taking directions from a female, but the route she pointed out did avoid the worst of the slums. Though they drove past a corner of the grim wall of the Foundling Hospital, on the whole the houses were respectable if not elegant. He turned into Great Ormond Street.

"I trust your friend Bubble will be available to walk my cattle?" It was like probing a sore tooth: he could not resist the distasteful subject of her acquaintance with the street boys.

"Do you mean to come in? I had not expected . . ."

"Surely you do not intend to leave me out here in the rain?"

"No, of course not. I had not thought . . . The mews is just across from our house, down that alley between the houses on the other side. I daresay they will take care of the horses.''

Bubble was absent but an equally grubby urchin, whom Miss Larkin addressed as Sammy, was sent scurrying after an ostler from the livery stables. The groom he fetched looked reasonably respectable. Philip grudgingly entrusted his precious pair to him. A few minutes later a neatly dressed maid ushered them into an entrance hall that smelled faintly of paint.

They were instantly and vociferously greeted by three small white terriers.

''Down, Flake, down, Drop, Goose.'' Her voice was imperative and the dogs obeyed at once. ''Where is Midnight? Oh, there you are, boy.''

The huge Newfoundland Philip remembered approached at a more dignified pace which failed to hide his eagerness. He leaned against Alison lovingly and Philip hurried to brace her.

''Thank you! I had forgot how heavy he is.'' She scratched the big black head.

''You guessed the significance of my horses' names, now let me guess your dogs'. Snowflake, Snowdrop and Snow Goose?''

Hearing their names the terriers set up a clamour again, as Alison nodded, laughing.

''Hush!'' she commanded.

In the sudden quiet the maid was heard to ask plaintively, ''Can I 'ave the umbrolly, if you please, sir. It's dripping on the floor.''

Philip handed it over and helped Miss Larkin out of her cloak. This operation was more complicated than it need have been because she was not concentrating. Her gaze was fixed on the umbrella stand, a strange-looking object that appeared to have toenails.

"It must be Aunt Zenobia's," she said uncertainly. "What is it?"

"It's an elephant's foot," announced a lean, elderly woman who joined them at that moment. Her voice was hushed and full of awe. "It's the foot of the elephant that stepped on poor Mr. Winkle."

There was a stunned silence.

"How...sad," said Miss Larkin.

Philip heard a tremor in her voice and did not dare catch her eye. It might be distress at her uncle's unusual end, but he had a feeling she was finding it as hard as he was not to burst into whoops of laughter.

"It's lovely to see you, Alison dear." The woman sounded brisk and practical now, as if she had never disclosed such a distressing demise.

"Oh Aunt Di, how I've missed you all!" They hugged each other. "Let me present Mr. Trevelyan, who was so kind as to bring me. Sir, this is Aunt Di—Miss Di, I suppose, since Aunt Polly is the eldest."

"How do you do, Miss Diana." Philip bowed.

"Di," she said firmly. "Thank you for bringing our girl to see us, Mr. Trevelyan. Bess, please tell the others that Miss Alison is come and then bring tea to the parlour. Now you know you are not allowed in the parlour. Stay."

After a startled moment, Philip realized that she was addressing the dogs. All humans present went into a room hung with bright green silk, embroidered with tigers and hummingbirds in black, orange, crimson and gold. Judging by Alison's dazed face, the room was newly decorated.

"It is a bit gaudy," said Miss Di apologetically. "Zenobia is so hard to dissuade when she has set her heart on something. We did manage to keep our bed-

chambers the way they were, just refurbished. Won't
you sit down, Mr. Trevelyan? Oh bother, Midnight has
come in. *She* will be annoyed, but he is used to being
allowed in here and when he is determined it is beyond
me to stop him.''

"Beyond anyone, I imagine, ma'am." Philip was
about to take a seat when two more elderly ladies entered. He was introduced to Aunt Cleo, plump and
somehow comfortable-looking, and Aunt Polly, who
seemed to drift rather than move of her own volition.

Alison hugged them both and they returned her embrace with fervour, obviously delighted to see her. At
last everyone was seated and the maid brought tea and
cakes. Mindful of Alison's remarks about her aunt's
superior baking, Philip took particular note of the
cakes, but upon tasting them determined that they were
not very good. He was wondering whether a polite lie
was in order when Alison set down her Bath bun, with
a large bite missing, and looked anxiously at Miss Cleo.

"Have you been ill, Aunt Cleo?"

The plump old lady's face crumpled. "No, dear, I
am very well," she said gruffly.

"We did not mean to tell you," said Miss Di, while
Miss Larkin—Aunt Polly—tried in vain to nod and
shake her head at one and the same time.

Philip could not reconcile these three harmless, and
presently unhappy, old biddies with the gang of guttersnipes Alison had mentioned. He had come intent
on investigating that gang, and now it seemed he was
about to be plunged into a domestic crisis.

Alison had moved to a footstool at Miss Di's feet
and was holding her hands. "Tell me," she urged.

"It's Zenobia . . ."

It was indeed. The door opened and a vast figure swathed in purple silk swam into the room, preceded by a waft of patchouli-scented air. Improbably red hair fringed a white, native-style turban in which was pinned the most enormous amethyst Philip had ever seen. He rose to his feet as the apparition surged forward.

"Aunt Zenobia, this is Mr. Trevelyan. He is a friend of Lady Emma."

"Pleasure to meet you, I'm sure," gasped Mrs. Winkle, sinking into a chair. "Just let me catch my breath. My umbrella split and I had to make a dash for it. Thank you, dear—yes, three spoons of sugar, that's right—how clever of you to remember. Well, Alison, let me look at you now." Her lack of breath seemed to have no effect on the flow of words.

Alison handed her the cup of tea and performed a graceful curtsy. She was wearing a gown of the palest lilac, high-necked and long-sleeved. A dark blue ribbon tied just beneath the bosom—Philip hastily averted his gaze, feeling his pulse quicken—trailed loose down the center of the skirt to the hem, so that the two ends fluttered when she moved.

"Hmm," said Mrs. Winkle dubiously. "Very elegant, I'm sure, but I like a bit of colour myself. A nice cherry stripe, or one of these new Scotch tartans would suit you to a T. Or better yet, I've plenty of stuffs put away that I brought home with me. The natives know what's what when it comes to pretty colours, I'll give them that."

"Lady Emma says a girl in her first Season must wear only pastels, Aunt, and white for evening parties."

"I'll have a word with Lady Emma before I leave, and we'll soon have you bang up to the nines, mark my words."

Though Alison blenched, the interest this comment aroused among the rest of the Misses Larkin had nothing to do with fashion.

"Leave?" queried Miss Di hesitantly.

"Mrs. Colonel Bowditch ain't happy in London. No one understands her, she says. Not that I pay much mind to such things, but I told her straight, I said, 'It's Cheltenham you want.' I've heard there's lots of us India hands living in Cheltenham, you see. So Mrs. Colonel Bowditch is thinking of leasing a house in Cheltenham, and I promised to go along to advise her." She heaved herself to her feet. "I'd best go get my ayah started on the packing, for we're off tomorrow. I'll be gone several weeks, but you needn't think I mean to leave you in the lurch, Alison. Ralph Osborne has promised to keep an eye on you for me."

Alison looked dismayed, but as Mrs. Winkle sailed out, Philip caught gleams of relief and hope in the eyes of the rest of her aunts. He was intrigued. What, he wondered, was going on here?

CHAPTER SIX

"WHAT IS GOING ON HERE?" asked Alison. "You are all in raptures."

"It's not that we are not grateful," said Aunt Di guiltily. "It is very pleasant not to have to worry over every last farthing."

"I never would have thought a fire in my chamber could make such a difference," put in Aunt Polly timidly, casting a scared glance at Mr. Trevelyan.

Alison looked at him. Though he must be bored, he had the courtesy to hide it with an expression of polite, but not excessive interest, a careful medium between inquisitiveness and indifference. She returned her attention to her troubled aunts.

"It's just that we have nothing to do," blurted out Aunt Cleo. "And the food is... well, I don't mean to boast but..."

"Atrocious," said Aunt Di firmly. "Why, the woman can scarcely boil an egg without cracking the shell. You see, Alison, Zenobia has hired a whole army of servants. It's all very well having a parlourmaid and a tweenie, and even a scullery maid, but the cook and the gardener are upsetting poor Cleo and Polly shockingly."

"And now that Zenobia is going away, we can turn them off," said Aunt Cleo in triumph.

"Oh, no, you cannot do that." Alison was adamant. "Only think how she will feel when she returns and learns that you have rejected her generosity. She will be sadly hurt."

"Zenobia's generosity is positively oppressive," muttered Aunt Di, rebelling.

"And think of the boys," Aunt Cleo reminded her. "If Polly can't grow her flowers and I can't bake, they will starve."

"I had not thought so far," Alison admitted. She noticed that Mr. Trevelyan, whose presence she had almost forgot was surprisingly alert. He caught her eye and promptly resumed his carefully indifferent expression. She was puzzled, but she had more important matters to consider. "Oh dear, if they have nothing to sell I am afraid they may turn to thievery. Aunt Polly, surely you can make use of the gardener?"

Aunt Polly looked terrified.

"You must not allow him to intimidate you. He should do the heavy digging and the dirty work under your direction. There is no reason why he should dictate what is grown and when it is picked. You will have time to experiment with other flowers, to find out which stay fresh in a basket and which sell well."

"I shall speak to the fellow," announced Aunt Di, "as soon as Zenobia is out of sight. You may trust me to deal with him. But what of the cook, Alison? It's no good saying she must be set to scrubbing pans, for there's the scullery maid to do that, and besides, I daresay it's beneath her dignity. She does run on about her dignity whenever Cleo tries to explain to her how to do things right."

"Yes, she must go or you will all fade away." Alison's grin was wicked. "I have it! You must persecute her, Aunt Cleo. Keep interfering and meddling and giving orders until her dignity cannot bear it. If she leaves of her own choice, Aunt Zenobia cannot be offended.''

''That's a splendid idea.'' Aunt Cleo was enthusiastic. ''I'll be that happy to get back to selling my...'' She stopped in alarm.

Aunt Zenobia stood in the doorway. ''There's not the least need to be wearing yourself out making a few pennies, Cleo,'' she said indulgently. ''You know if there's any little thing you want you must just ask me.''

''It's the boys! We are taken care of, but they may starve for want of those few pennies.''

''How much do they make? Not more than a few rupees a week between the lot of them, I wager. I'll be glad to give that much for you to hand over to them. I've got plenty.''

Mr. Trevelyan's voice came as a shock to everyone. ''I beg your pardon for interfering, ladies,'' he said, dropping his pose of indifference, ''but I must point out the advantages of having the boys earn their money. Surely it is preferable that they should learn to work rather than living on charity?''

''To be sure, but I don't care to have people thinking my sisters have to work for their living when I'm rich as the Begum of Oudh.''

''Then turn over the entire proceeds of the enterprise to your street hawkers, or better, put some in a fund for them against illness and other emergencies.''

Aunt Zenobia seemed inclined to argue. ''But—'' she began.

''It is time we were on our way,'' he added quickly, silencing her. ''I am happy to have made your acquaintance, ladies.''

Alison found herself ruthlessly removed from the bosom of her family.

"Heavens," she sighed as Mr. Trevelyan handed her up into the tilbury. She leaned back against the green leather seat. "To think I imagined all our troubles were over when Aunt Zenobia appeared like a fairy godmother. Thank you so much, sir, for your suggestions. I was afraid you would be shocked when you found out about the boys."

"To tell the truth," he admitted sheepishly, "I quite expected to discover your aunt running a gang of thieves and pickpockets."

"Aunt Cleo?" Alison gaped at him, then collapsed in whoops. "You cannot be serious!" she gasped through her laughter.

"Alas, I am. It is partly your fault, for you used the word gang. Mostly it is because I am a member of the Select Committee investigating crime in the city. We have uncovered a number of what are called 'flash-houses,' run by people who live quite respectable lives to all outward appearances."

What was a flash-house? she wondered. Obviously something utterly disreputable—she had better not ask. "Select Committee?" she queried instead.

"A parliamentary body set up for a specific purpose."

"That would explain it. I was puzzled once or twice when you spoke of having to be at the House. It seemed an odd way to say at home. You are a Member of Parliament?"

"I am, Miss Alison."

"Lord Fane sits in the House of Lords. He did not mention any committees, though."

"Alas, I am a mere commoner, though naturally some of our committee members are peers. Lord Fane called on you?"

"Yes, twice, and the second time we were at home. He is prodigious agreeable and gentlemanly. You were quite right, I did not need to say anything, only to listen demurely."

"Now that I find quite impossible to imagine," he said with a twinkle in his eye. "I need not warn you to say nothing to him of Bubble and Squeak, and what was the other name?"

"Tarry Joe. His mother thinks his father was a sailor. No, I fear Lord Fane would not understand. Indeed, Lady Emma made me promise not to mention my aunts to him."

"By the way, I believe I have solved the riddle of your aunts' names." Mr. Trevelyan looked pleased with himself. "Miss Di is Dido, is she not? I guessed when she objected to being called Diana. Zenobia gave me a clue, and Cleo is Cleopatra, I take it? Polly had me puzzled, since that is usually a nickname for Mary, until I thought of Hippolyta, the Amazon. All tragic queens from classical history or myth."

Alison was impressed. "That is much cleverer than guessing the origin of the dogs' names. My grandfather was a classical scholar with a taste for the tragical. You need not think he discriminated against females, for my papa was called Hector after the prince of Troy slain by Achilles."

"A classical scholar? That is unusual for a . . ." He paused in confusion.

"For a Cit?"

"I beg your pardon. I ought not to have said such a thing." Mr. Trevelyan was annoyed. Alison suspected he prided himself on his tact.

"But you did not say the word. I did." She smiled forgivingly. "And it is the truth, whether stated or not. Unfortunately he was a better classicist than merchant, and since my father died young it was left to Aunt Zenobia to recoup the family fortunes. I am prodigious grateful to her, of course, but I do hope she will not continue to throw the rest of my aunts into high fidgets!"

"At least they are safe for the next few weeks, so you can enjoy your Season without worry."

Alison doubted that anything could prevent her enjoying the Season. Lord Fane's visit—which had lasted nearly three-quarters of an hour—had set the seal on her expectations of having a wonderful time.

One slight shadow on her pleasure did not materialize: Aunt Zenobia failed to arrive with a trunk full of Indian fabrics. A note from Aunt Di next day informed her that Mrs. Winkle had been with great difficulty persuaded that Lady Emma knew best what a young lady ought to wear. She had gone off to Cheltenham with Mrs. Colonel Bowditch, leaving everyone guiltily breathing easier for her absence. Alison was able to look forward with unalloyed anticipation to her first formal dinner party.

To her disappointment, Lord Fane had not been invited to this event. Lady Emma was tempted, since four—the two of them plus Philip and Robert—was an awkward number and she wanted to ask Bella, whose husband was out of town. Another gentleman would be useful. However, she decided that an intimate party of six might seem so particular as to make his lordship take fright.

Her seating arrangements were still on her mind when Mr. Ralph Osborne called on the morning of the dinner party.

He was diffident. "I do not mean to intrude on your ladyship," he said, on being shown into the drawing-room. "I promised to keep an eye on Miss Alison, and since Mrs. Winkle left Town today, I thought I had best introduce myself."

Alison wanted to protest that she did not need an eye kept on her, especially by the man her aunt wanted her to marry. Lady Emma spoke first.

"But I remember you well, Mr. Osborne. Will you not be seated? I was grateful for your assistance in solving one or two little differences of opinion with Mrs. Winkle."

He grinned, and Alison had to admit that he was handsome, in an exotic way, with his blond hair and tanned face. His tall, broad-shouldered form had towered over them until he sat down. It was almost a pity that he was so old, and untitled, and unexciting.

"Mrs. Winkle's notions are sometimes . . . original, shall we say, but she is a thoroughly good-hearted, generous woman. I owe my success in India entirely to her husband."

Lady Emma asked him one or two questions about India. Alison, having heard the answers from her aunt before she had come to Mayfair, concentrated on a tricky bit of needlework. Her attention was swiftly brought back to the conversation when, surprised and annoyed, she heard her chaperon issue an invitation to dine with them that evening.

"It will only be a small party of friends," Lady Emma went on. "I beg your pardon for the short notice."

"I am honoured, my lady, and I shall be delighted to accept. I must be off now. I shall see you this evening, Miss Alison." He smiled at her in an odiously fatherly way and departed.

Her astonished gaze brought a tinge of pink to Lady Emma's cheeks.

"He is amazingly gentlemanlike," she said, sounding defensive, "and his anecdotes are both interesting and amusing. Our dinner party needs a counterbalance to Robert's poetic attitude. Bella is not so high in the instep that she will object."

"But I object," said Alison crossly. "It is bad enough knowing that Aunt Zenobia wishes me to marry him without falling over him at every turn. Keep an eye on me, indeed!"

"It is kind in him to take a personal interest." Lady Emma was equally put out. "He might be satisfied with merely paying our bills."

"Paying our bills?"

"Yes, I send them all to him. Remember he is Mrs. Winkle's man of business."

"Aunt Zenobia told me they were to be sent to her. How humiliating to have Mr. Osborne informed of every set of buttons or pair of stockings I purchase!"

"If I do not feel humiliated, there is no need for you to do so," Lady Emma snapped. "As long as you do not purchase a diamond tiara, I would wager he will look only at the totals, not at every item. He appears to be a gentleman of considerable sensitivity and discretion. Pray do not stir up a tempest in a teapot."

Alison apologized, knowing she had been unreasonable. It was not that she had taken Mr. Osborne in dislike, precisely. Perhaps she was afraid that his proprietorial air might discourage Lord Fane, but after all, they were not likely to meet.

She greeted Mr. Osborne in her usual friendly manner when he arrived that evening, but it was Mr. Trevelyan she was truly glad to see. In the course of their visit to Great Ormond Street, he had climbed from the status of an agreeable acquaintance to that of friend. It was hard to believe she had found him forbidding at first. She wanted to talk to him about meeting Lady Emma's parents, the Earl and Countess of Edgehill, on whom they had called a few hours earlier and who had been amazingly kind.

Lady Emma had warned her that, in such a small company, conversation must be general. On her best behaviour, she therefore found it impossible to speak privately with Mr. Trevelyan before or during dinner.

The gentlemen did not sit long over the port afterwards. When they joined the ladies in the drawing-room, the Honourable Robert Gilchrist took the place beside Alison on the sofa before she could invite Mr. Trevelyan to join her.

"I have finished my sonnet," he declared in throbbing tones. "I shall read it to you."

"Thank you, sir," she said uncertainly, looking to Lady Emma for guidance.

"You may read it to all of us, Robert," his sister ordered.

He did not appear at all abashed, but stood up, struck a pose and cleared his throat. Relishing the audience, he declaimed,

"Her eyes are like the summer skies,
Albeit stars do dwell therein."

"Very pretty," applauded Lady Fairfield.
"Don't interrupt, Bella," he admonished her.

"Her curls are midnight. In both lies
A magic that makes my head spin."

Alison giggled, and clapped a hand to her mouth. "I beg your pardon, sir."

"What do you find so amusing?" he demanded sulkily.

"Not your verse," she tried to appease him, "which is very clever. You must blame my wretched imagination. I had a vision of your head twirling around like a spinning top. Pray do read on, sir."

The unfeeling laughter of his sisters and Mr. Trevelyan did nothing to diminish Mr. Gilchrist's indignation. Alison saw Ralph Osborne's lips twitch and was grateful to him for not adding fuel to the flames. It was Lady Fairfield who came to the rescue.

"I believe I shall try out your spinet, Emma," she announced, appearing unconscious of the unfortunate coincidence of the instrument's name, with Alison's spinning top flight of fancy, "if you have any simple music. I have not played this age. Come, Robert, you shall turn the pages for me."

Still sulky, he obeyed, and Mr. Trevelyan moved to take his seat.

"I thought you would be in raptures to have a sonnet dedicated to you," he said teasingly to Alison under cover of a laborious sonatina.

"It *is* flattering, and the poem began very prettily. It was wicked of me to hurt his feelings so, but I did not mean to."

"Wickeder of the rest of us to laugh. Do not take it to heart. I have the impression that you have been bursting to tell me something ever since I arrived."

"Proper young ladies do not burst," she admonished. "Yes, I want to tell you about going to see Lord and Lady Edgehill. Their house is so very grand that I was quite nervous, especially as Lady Emma told me they do not approve of her acting as a chaperon. But they were not at all high in the instep. In fact, they were excessively obliging. Only think, when we were about to leave, Lady Edgehill asked Lady Emma what date she wanted their ballroom for my come-out ball!"

"And did she set a date?" he asked with polite interest.

"Oh, do not be so impassive! You are teasing me again," she said as he laughed. "I never expected to have my very own ball. Is it not splendid? You will come, will you not?"

"If I am invited."

"You are odious this evening. Lady Emma would sooner forget to invite her own brother than you."

"Then may I hope to stand up with you for a waltz?"

"I did not mean to fish for that," she said uncertainly.

"If I had thought it of you, I'd not have asked."

"Then thank you, sir, I shall look forward to it."

Lady Fairfield left shortly thereafter, exhausted, she claimed, by her musical efforts. She enlisted her brother, over his objections, to escort her home. Mr. Osborne, who had been conversing quietly with his hostess, took this as a signal to depart, and Mr. Trevelyan went with him, offering to drive him home. Lady Emma yawned delicately.

"You have had a busy day. I expect you are as ready to retire as I am."

Alison did not feel in the least sleepy, but she acquiesced. As they made their way upstairs, she said, "I am sorry to have offended Mr. Gilchrist."

"Do not let it trouble you, my dear. I know you did not mean to laugh at that inauspicious moment. Tomorrow I shall teach you how to turn a misplaced laugh into a cough, for there is no denying that gentlemen have a way of making one laugh unintentionally. It will not do to offend a gentleman of more consequence than my little brother."

"Oh no!" Alison's eyes were round with horror.

"In the meantime," Lady Emma soothed her, "if you have cured Robert of his imagined tendre for you, we shall go on much more comfortably."

"It was poor thanks for his writing a poem about me. I daresay such a compliment will never come my way again. You do not suppose he will persuade Lady Edgehill not to let me have my ball in their house?"

"He will not try, and if he did Mama would not pay the least heed. You may sleep tranquil." She yawned again and disappeared into her chamber.

Alison was sure she was too excited to sleep at all. She was to have a proper come-out ball, and Mr. Trevelyan had already reserved a waltz. It only remained for Lord Fane to request another for her happiness to be complete. She felt for his card, dog-eared now, beneath her pillow.

Carter came in to see if she needed anything, and snuffed her candle. She was asleep within minutes.

CHAPTER SEVEN

"ARE YOU SURE YOU ARE quite warm enough, Miss Larkin?"

Alison had a delicious feeling that if she said no, Lord Fane would strip off his greatcoat and wrap it round her. He was the very soul of chivalry. However, though a blustery wind tossed the bare branches of the elm trees in the Park, she was not at all cold.

"Thanks to your forethought in providing this rug, my lord, I am perfectly comfortable."

"You must not be nervous if my horses are a little restive today. They do not care for this wind."

"I have perfect confidence in your driving, sir."

"I am known as something of a whip," he agreed with a modest air. "Of course I would not subject a lady to the indignity and danger of riding in a sporting rig, such as that high-perch phaeton you will see over there." He indicated a nearby vehicle. "Ah, it is Kilmore. A rackety fellow, I fear."

Alison wisely decided not to say that the high-perch phaeton looked as if it would be great fun to ride in. Lady Emma had told her that Lord Fane was a high stickler, so if he said that such a carriage was unsuitable for a lady he must be right. She wondered who the female was sitting up so high beside the rackety Kilmore. Not a lady, presumably. She hastily averted her gaze, but not before Kilmore had noticed her interest and raised his dark eyebrows with an amused smile.

She was slightly embarrassed—and very much intrigued.

Lord Fane had an extensive acquaintance among the tón, and a large proportion of them seemed to have braved the wind to drive or ride in Hyde Park at the fashionable hour. He was constantly greeting people. Several times he drew up his carriage to speak to more particular friends, to whom he introduced Alison.

He presented her as Lady Emma Grant's protégée, and everyone seemed to accept that as sufficient credentials. There was one elderly lady who went off muttering, "Larkin? Larkin?" to herself, but if his lordship heard he did not mention it. Like the rest, he apparently assumed that Lady Emma would never dream of chaperoning a young lady without an impeccable family tree.

Alison was well aware that if the gossipmongers ever discovered her humble background she would be ostracized. But for the moment, reassured that she was accepted, she was enjoying herself immensely.

"I believe I am the envy of every buck in sight," said Lord Fane, with what Alison considered justifiable satisfaction, as he turned his horse towards the gate. "I trust you will give me the pleasure of your company driving in the Park again in the near future?"

"Thank you, my lord, you are very kind."

"I must be grateful to Trevelyan for making us acquainted, thus enabling me to steal a march upon those rivals who will swarm about you as soon as you are properly presented to Society. Speaking of which, I received an invitation to your ball this morning. Dare I beg you to reserve two dances for me, before your card is quite filled up?''

"Oh yes, sir, that will be delightful.''

"You are unengaged for the supper dance, perhaps?''

Breathless, Alison nodded. This was an honour indeed!

"Then I insist that you write me down for it.'' His lordship chuckled to show that his insistence was a joke and not unpardonable rudeness.

A few minutes later he helped her down from the carriage in Park Street and escorted her to the front door. Refusing an invitation to step in, he took his leave.

"I shall hold you to your promise, mind. You must write it down immediately lest you forget.''

"I shall not forget!'' Alison vowed. She asked the footman, Henry, who opened the door where Lady Emma was to be found.

"Her ladyship's in the drawing-room, miss.'' He grinned at her. "You've had good news, looks like?''

She nodded, beaming, and sped to the drawing-room. Lady Emma looked round as she entered.

"Such a famous thing, ma'am. Lord Fane has engaged me for the supper dance!'' She realized that a gentleman, seated with his back to her, was rising politely. "Oh, I beg your pardon, I did not know anyone... How do you do, sir. Is it not beyond anything great?''

Mr. Trevelyan bowed and said mockingly, "Beyond anything. I'm off, Emma. I shall bring you the book I spoke of in the morning, early, after my ride.'' His face a mask of boredom, he nodded to Alison and strode from the room.

Crestfallen, she dropped into a chair.

"I am sorry Mr. Trevelyan was not pleased for me," she said plaintively.

"I daresay he is feeling a trifle downpin for some reason quite unconnected with you. So Lord Fane has done his duty, has he?"

Alison laughed. "I do not mean to boast but I believe he thought it a pleasure. He claimed that all the gentlemen in the Park envied him for driving me in his carriage. Was not that a pretty thing to say?"

"Most gratifying."

"There was one gentleman—at least I suppose he is a gentleman. Lord Fane said he was a rackety fellow. Kilmore is his name, do you know him?"

"Lord Kilmore? Yes, we are acquainted. I believe I sent him an invitation to the ball."

"You did? I thought perhaps he was not quite respectable."

Lady Emma shrugged. "He is received everywhere. His manners are charming, and he is always ready to oblige by standing up with young ladies who are not in great demand."

"Wallflowers? I hope I shall not be one. Lord Fane did ask for a second dance as well so I have three taken already. Unless Mr. Trevelyan means to cry off his?"

"Why ever should he do that?"

"He looked at me as if he did not like me, just now."

"Nonsense, my dear. His mind was elsewhere. Besides he is by far too much the gentleman to do such a shocking thing. You may count on four dances, for my father has offered to lead you out for the first set since the ball is in his house."

"Lord Edgehill?" Alison's eyes grew round. "I do not deserve such an honour."

"He, too, considers it a pleasure. A 'fetching puss' was how he described you to me. My parents have both taken quite a liking to you—I know you will strive to earn their approval. Mama means to come to our tea-party tomorrow. Your aunt is to be relied upon to supply the cakes and biscuits, is she not?"

"Oh yes, ma'am. She was so pleased and proud when you agreed to let her provide them. I expect she will be up all night baking. You can count on Aunt Cleo."

ALISON REMAINED confident of this claim until approximately half past nine the next morning, when Aunt Di arrived, accompanied by Midnight. Admitted to the breakfast parlour, where Alison and Lady Emma were discussing the plans for the day, she burst into tears.

The acutely embarrassed footman who had let her in waved helplessly at Midnight. "She says as she's miss's auntie, my lady, and I can't stop the dog."

"You acted perfectly correctly, Henry," Lady Emma assured him, her wary gaze on the dog, while Alison sat the visitor down at the table, passed her a handkerchief and poured her a cup of tea.

"What is wrong, Aunt Di?" she asked in alarm. "Is someone ill?"

"Cleo wishes she was dead," sniffed the miserable old lady. "That wretched maid Zenobia *would* hire left the kitchen door open and the terriers gobbled everything in sight."

"The cakes for the party?"

"The cakes for the party. I'm so sorry, Alison dear, I don't rightly know what to say."

"It was not your fault, Aunt Di." She glanced for help at Lady Emma, whose eyes never wavered from Midnight.

The dog was advancing on her, tail waving gently, nose quivering, a plea in his deep-set eyes. Lady Emma involuntarily reached for a muffin.

"Midnight, behave yourself," said Aunt Di sharply, recalled to her surroundings.

"We try to avoid feeding him at the table," Alison explained.

"But *he* did not steal the cakes. Is there nothing left?" her ladyship asked, tearing off a piece of the muffin and holding it out in a slightly nervous hand.

Midnight took the tidbit from her with a delicate nibble. He laid his heavy black head on her lavender cambric lap and looked up at her in adoration. She fed him another morsel as Aunt Di answered gloomily.

"Nothing but crumbs, my lady. Cleo ran out to buy more flour and sugar and such, but she won't have time to bake everything again, not with one oven and one pair of hands."

There was silence as they contemplated the disaster. Midnight ate the last scrap of muffin, gave Lady Emma's hand a polite lick and followed his nose to the sideboard, under which he stretched out for a snooze surrounded by the heavenly aroma of bacon and eggs.

"I doubt my kitchen is as large as yours," said Lady Emma with a sigh. "I shall have Cook do what she can, and I daresay Gunter's will have something, though they make a sad fuss if you do not give them adequate notice."

"Gunter's?" Mr. Trevelyan stepped into the breakfast room. "Here is the book I promised you, Emma.

Good morning, Miss Di, Miss Alison. What is this talk of Gunter's?''

Three voices explained at once. He seemed to have no difficulty untangling the tale.

"If my chef cannot provide sufficient confections for a tea-party at five hours notice, I shall want to know why. Send your footman round with your orders, Emma. Now, Miss Di, may I offer you a ride home?''

"Thank you, sir, but I brought the dog. I was so flustered I didn't think to take a hackney."

"One of the culprits, eh?'' He caught sight of the big dog under the sideboard. "No, it's Midnight. I have every confidence in Midnight's behaving like a gentleman in my carriage.''

Hearing his name, the Newfoundland lurched to his feet and paced over to greet Mr. Trevelyan.

"Will you really take him in the tilbury?'' Alison asked with a giggle. "I hope he will not overset you. I shall watch you driving down the street. Sir, I do thank you for coming to our rescue, and for taking Aunt Di home.''

"My pleasure, Miss Alison.''

"Poor Aunt Cleo must be sadly disappointed,'' she said with a sigh.

He smiled at her. "Perhaps I can do something about that as well. Will your aunt like, do you think, to supervise my kitchen staff while they bake to her receipts?''

She clasped her hands, eyes shining. "You would let her?''

"I daresay my chef will leave in a dudgeon but I shan't regard that.''

"He will? I hope you are roasting me! Aunt Cleo will be *aux anges*. Give her my love, Aunt Di, and tell her I shall come tomorrow to tell her how everyone enjoyed her pastries.''

From the window she watched as Mr. Trevelyan courteously assisted Aunt Di into the carriage and with a snap of his fingers summoned Midnight to lie at his feet. The urchin holding the horses' heads let go—she noticed with surprise that it was Tarry Joe—and Spaniard and Conqueror trotted off.

In his teasing way, Mr. Trevelyan was as chivalrous as Lord Fane. And she seemed to be in favour again, though she had no notion what she had done the day before to lose his good opinion. She sighed deeply, though she was not sure why.

Lady Emma returned from dispatching Henry with her order for Mr. Trevelyan's chef, and sank into her chair.

''Pour me a cup of tea, there's a dear. What an exhausting morning!''

Alison complied. ''I did not know Mr. Trevelyan had a large house. At least, I suppose he does as he had no doubts as to his kitchen being adequate.''

''Yes, the house is a good size. In fact, he has a small ballroom, and if Mama had not offered hers I should have asked the loan of his. It has not been used since his younger sister married, though he often entertains his parliamentary colleagues with dinners. I have acted as hostess for him on occasion, when he wished to invite their wives also.''

''He has sisters?''

''Two, married to country gentlemen, and two brothers. One is a naval captain and the other a clergyman.''

''How odd. Somehow I always thought of him as . . . rather alone.''

"He is closer to his family than to anyone else, but he sees little of them during the parliamentary terms. I am fortunate in being a sort of surrogate sister, having known him so long."

Alison found she was envious of that good fortune.

At half past two that afternoon, a pair of liveried footmen turned up at the servants' entrance bearing napkin-covered trays. When they departed, Lady Emma's Henry went with them, and all three returned ten minutes later with another three trays. It took them one more trip to bring all the confections from Mr. Trevelyan's house just round the corner in Green Street. Shortly thereafter, silver platters and cake-stands laden with biscuits and pastries and petits fours began to make their appearance in the drawing-room.

All Aunt Cleo's favourite receipts were there. Thanks to Mr. Trevelyan she had after all been able to do her part to make her niece's début successful.

Two of the first guests to arrive were Lady Witherington and her pretty blond daughter. Alison and Lady Emma had called on them since the episode at Schomberg House, and Alison was strongly drawn to the lively and amiable Fanny Witherington. The feeling appeared to be mutual. Alison was most relieved to have a friend to lend her confidence in the face of the rest of the guests, a dozen debutantes and their critical mamas.

Fanny was also one of the last to leave.

"Their opinions are about equally divided," she whispered to Alison as her mother and Lady Emma exchanged compliments. "Half of them will not dare let their daughters go near you for fear of comparisons in your favour. The other half realize that the gentlemen will flock to your side and that their daughters may profit from the overflow. If you see what I mean.''

"I see, but do you really think so?"

"I am certain of it. Fortunately, Mama is one of the latter group."

Alison laughed and shook her head. "Fustian. I am as likely to profit from your overflow as you from mine."

"We shall see. Your ball is the day before mine, so we can compare. I must go, Mama is calling. Oof, I can scarcely move, I have eaten so much. Do not forget that I shall call for you tomorrow afternoon to walk in the Park."

As soon as the last guest disappeared, Lady Emma turned to Alison in triumph.

"Seven invitations!" she announced, "and Lady Witherington wanted to know where I found such delicious cakes."

CHAPTER EIGHT

"AND LADY WITHERINGTON wanted to know where Lady Emma found such delicious cakes," Alison reported to Aunt Cleo, who beamed with pride. "She invited me to Fanny's ball, too. It is the day after mine."

"Do you think," said Aunt Polly, aghast at her own daring, "that you could use my flowers to decorate the ballroom? I do so want to help."

Alison kissed her. "Lady Edgehill is seeing to the decorations. I shall have to ask her."

Aunt Polly's face fell. "Oh no, dear, you mustn't do that. I thought your Lady Emma was making the arrangements. She seems such a kind person."

"Lady Emma told her mama all about us, so you need not fear she will be shocked." Alison could tell by the unwonted spate of words that the opportunity to contribute meant a great deal to her aunt. "I shall certainly ask her about the flowers. Oh, and I nearly forgot to tell you, Aunt Cleo—Lady Edgehill came to tea yesterday, and she sent her compliments on your baking."

The very next day, to his own surprised disapproval, Mr. Philip Trevelyan found himself offering to convey Miss Hippolyta Larkin to see the Edgehills' ballroom and consult with the countess.

"You will be gentle with her, will you not?" Alison begged him, her pixie face anxious. "She is sadly timid."

"I rarely indulge in fisticuffs with elderly ladies," he said drily, somewhat affronted at her lack of confidence in him.

"You know that is not what I mean. I wish I could accompany you, but Lady Emma insists that I go for a fitting of my ball gown."

"I trust it is to be tartan, to please Mrs. Winkle, or have you chosen cherry stripes?"

"*That* is what I mean. If you speak to Aunt Polly in your teasing way, she will not know where to look."

"Miss Larkin will come to no harm at my hands or my tongue, I promise you. And I shall guard her from that dragon, Lady Edgehill, with my life."

"You will always be joking," she said crossly, but he thought he saw relief in her blue eyes.

Was he really such an ogre in those same eyes? How had young Robert described them—stars shining in the midday sky, or some such thing. He was not so far off at that.

Philip was amused to find that her aunts thought of him not as an ogre but as a hero. He was the gentleman who had saved the day for Cleo's cakes. Aunt Polly went with him quite happily, if wordlessly, and seemed to enjoy the ride in his tilbury.

Lady Edgehill, a tall, stately woman who dwarfed Polly, was expecting them and greeted her graciously. She showed them into the ballroom.

"My daughter tells me... Why, whatever is the matter, Miss Larkin?"

Philip swung round in alarm. Big, silent tears were welling up in Aunt Polly's faded eyes and her mouth was a picture of tragedy. He took her hands in his, noting for the first time the ridges and bumps. His mother's hands had been twisted by rheumatism.

"What is troubling you, ma'am?" he asked gently.

"I thought the room would be smaller. I haven't got anywhere near enough flowers. I did want to do something for Alison," she wailed.

Lady Edgehill looked as if she was sorry she had ever involved herself in the business. Her sniff was a masterpiece of reproach.

"We shall work something out," Philip promised. "What flowers do you have?"

"Daffodils and narcissus and jonquils."

"Spring," he said, "Alison's—Miss Alison's favourite season." He glanced about the room. The walls were cream, picked out in gold, with green-velvet-draped window bays along one side and matching conversation bays opposite. In the piers between the bays there were niches holding vaguely classical statuettes. At the far end was a small dais for the musicians. Tradition dictated that this should be hidden by banks of flowers. "Greenery, spring greenery everywhere. Not evergreens, not potted palms, but fresh leaves from the country. There must be something out already."

"It would be different," said Lady Edgehill cautiously.

"And then, ma'am, you fill the niches with spring flowers. Vases of daffodils, blowing their trumpets to announce the arrival of spring."

"Heavens, you sound like Robert!"

"And narcissus and jonquils," Aunt Polly added, hope in her eyes.

"Are the narcissus scented? Only think, my lady, of the delicate perfume greeting the jaded nostrils of the ton."

"Until they have been dancing for half an hour," she grumbled, but she was convinced. "It *will* be different."

Philip drove the joyful and touchingly grateful Miss Larkin home. She reminded him of his mother, now that he had seen a connection. Mrs. Trevelyan, though not shy, had had the same somewhat vague air, and she had enjoyed dabbling in gardening. He dredged up memories of the flowers she had grown, and kept Aunt Polly entertained until they reached Great Ormond Street.

"I shall see if I can get you some seeds," he offered.

She was too overwhelmed to thank him.

His next impulse was to drive straight to Park Street to tell Alison of his intervention in her aunt's behalf. He was half-way there when he decided it would look too much like bragging. She would find out soon enough anyway.

Instead he went to Gentleman Jackson's Boxing Saloon for a bout of fisticuffs. Philip was well versed in the Corinthian sports of boxing, shooting, driving and riding, and his skill at fencing was superior. He did not consider himself a Corinthian, any more than he was a gamester because he occasionally took a hand at piquet, whist or faro. Leading a young lady into a country dance or cotillion, lending his talents to his country in a government post, all these were aspects of being a gentleman. He might enjoy some aspects more than others, but he had been bred up to do his duty, and occasional boredom was the price one paid for the advantage of superior birth.

Boredom? His thoughts arrested on that word. He had rarely suffered that particular malady since Miss Alison Larkin had entered his life.

He doubted she knew the meaning of the word.

AT THAT PRECISE MOMENT, Alison might have disputed the point. Shivering in her shift while Lady Emma and the modiste argued over the propriety of the décolletage of her ball gown, she wished for a fairy godmother's magic wand. If only all her new dresses might appear in instantaneous perfection, instead of the tedious business of tapes and pins and endless fittings.

She chided herself for ingratitude. High neck or low neck, the gown was heavenly—except that she did not want to shock Lord Fane.

"I should prefer it a little less décolleté, if you please," she requested.

If Philip Trevelyan knew he would tease her for her desire to indulge his lordship's taste for decorum. It was only natural, she thought indignantly, to want to please the gentleman she hoped to marry.

He really had been most particular in his attentions, and she was not yet even properly out.

She spent the rest of the day with Fanny Witherington. They had a delicious cose about ball gowns and beaux and favourite novels, on all of which subjects their views coincided exactly. Nothing could be more delightful, they agreed, than to have a lord at one's feet professing undying love. By the time the Witheringtons' carriage took Alison home, her head was a-whirl with romantic fancies the more vivid for being shared.

She was eager to tell Lady Emma about her afternoon. Remembering how disapproving Philip had been when she rushed in with her news, she paused in the doorway to make sure her chaperon was alone. She heard Philip's dry voice and was glad she had hesitated.

"Ever since she came to you, our lives have been full of turmoil. I only hope that whatever happens next does not turn her Season into an utter disaster."

Softly she withdrew. Tears stung her eyes as she trailed up the stairs to her chamber. She dashed them away. She would not allow the wretched man to overset her. It was ridiculous that one person should be able to confuse her so, swinging her emotions from friendship and gratitude to fury and chagrin. She had to admit that it hurt her to be at outs with him.

Lady Emma, coming up to change for dinner, knocked on her door. To judge by the placidity of her expression, she did not take Philip's warning seriously.

"Did you have a pleasant time with Miss Witherington? I must tell you what came of your aunt's visit to my mother. Philip was unable to resist boasting about it."

"Boasting?"

"It seems your aunt was sadly dismayed by the size of the ballroom." She explained Philip's solution and went on, "He was disgracefully pleased with himself. And he confessed to having developed quite a tendre for Miss Polly Larkin. She reminds him of his late mother."

Alison did not know what to say. As she changed her dress, she puzzled over the words she had heard. Perhaps he had been joking, as he must have been when he said he was fond of Aunt Polly. It was often difficult to tell when he was serious. Now she would have to be grateful to him again. Drat the man!

THE DAY OF THE BALL arrived at last. From the moment they met at the breakfast table, Lady Emma poured a stream of reminders into Alison's ears.

"Never dance with the same gentleman more than twice. That is your only good reason for refusing a request if you are not already engaged. Unless the gentleman is obviously foxed, of course. Return to me between sets, or if that should be difficult, to Mama or Bella, or Lady Witherington. Remember that though we do not hope for Almack's, the patronesses can ruin you with a word. Sally Jersey has a sharp tongue and Mrs. Drummond-Burrell is shockingly high in the instep. I need not tell you, I feel sure, not to be tongue-tied, but for heaven's sake, Alison, do not talk of your aunts."

By the time Carter carefully placed the ball gown over her head, under Lady Emma's watchful eye, Alison was decidedly nervous. She would never remember all the rules. It was comforting to know that as well as her chaperon, Philip would be there to advise her.

She must stop thinking of him as Philip or one of these days she would forget to address him as Mr. Trevelyan.

There was a tap at the door. Carter answered it and a moment later returned with two posies: pink rosebuds from Lord Fane and lilies of the valley from Mr. Trevelyan. Alison was in an agony of indecision.

"What shall I do?" she cried. She held up the delicate spray of lilies of the valley against the white satin and silver net of her gown, then raised them to her nose and breathed deeply of the sweet fragrance. "They both must have been grown in a greenhouse. These go much better with my dress, but it is excessively flattering of Lord Fane to send roses and I should hate to offend him."

"A fearful dilemma," Lady Emma agreed, amused. "While you are trying to decide, I shall dress."

Alison went with her and Carter to her dressing-room. Lady Emma's ball gown was an elegant creation of sea-green satin with a lace overdress like white sea foam. She had been wearing more youthful colours recently and, watching Carter arrange her fair hair in ringlets, Alison was amazed at how young and pretty her chaperon looked.

"I hope you mean to dance tonight," she said impulsively.

"Why yes, I believe I shall, if any kind gentleman should ask me. It would not do in general, but Mama is in some sort your sponsor tonight. Have you yet decided the vexing question of which flowers to carry?"

Alison was relieved of the necessity of choosing when Henry carried up a third nosegay of white rosebuds.

"It is from Lord Edgehill," she gasped, reading the card. "How very kind of your papa. I had best take these, had I not? Neither Lord Fane nor Mr. Trevelyan can be hurt then, since Lord Edgehill is such a venerable gentleman."

"Very true." Lady Emma sniffed the roses she too had received from her father, then set them down and picked up another posy, one of two already on her dressing-table.

Alison wondered who the favoured blooms were from but decided it would be impertinent to ask.

The flowers reminded her of Aunt Polly, and she could not help worrying lest the terriers had decided to dig up the garden and destroy the decorations for the ballroom. As soon as they reached the Edgehills' house, she asked the countess if the daffodils had arrived safely.

"Come and see," said her ladyship, leading the way. "It was most extraordinary," she added to her daughter. "The flowers were brought by a troop of ragamuffins, and one of them had the gall to ask to see the room where Miss Alison would be dancing! Of course Jeffries said no, and twenty minutes later one of the footmen caught them peering in through the windows! He chased them off and nothing seems to be missing."

Alison was glad the boys had managed to peek at the ballroom. The elegant splendour of gilt-and-crystal chandeliers illuminated a rustic bower. Spring greenery was massed around the dais and wreathed the walls, while here and there slender vases of daffodils and narcissus added a touch of delicate beauty.

"Most original," Lady Emma approved.

Before she had time to admire the scene properly, Alison was whisked out again and found herself part of a receiving line headed by the earl and countess. She lost count of the number of times she curtsied to matrons in feathers and diamonds, gentlemen elegant in black and white or foppishly arrayed in brighter hues. Swarms of young ladies in pastels eyed her with curiosity, some friendly, some condescending, some shy.

All these fashionable people had gathered in her honour, she realized with a sense of shock. She, Alison Larkin of Great Ormond Street, was actually making her début in Society.

It was a great relief to see Fanny Witherington, who winked at her and whispered, "Is it a frightful ordeal? I shall be going through the agony tomorrow."

At last Philip Trevelyan appeared, an equally welcome sight. He smiled down at her.

"Tonight we have the elf, not the leprechaun. Enchanting! I hope you have not forgot my dance?"

"Of course not, sir. Thank you so much for the flowers."

"Those are Lord Fane's, I take it."

She was glad to be able to deny his assumption. "No, he sent pink roses. Yours were quite the prettiest, but these are from Lord Edgehill, you see."

Before he could respond, the person behind him interrupted in a deep, lazy voice. "Would that I might have had the honour of having my offering rejected in favour of our worthy host's."

Alison looked up into the admiring eyes of a dark, handsome gentleman she recognized.

"Lord Kilmore, Alison," said Lady Emma. "Allow me to present my protégée, Kilmore: Miss Alison Larkin."

He bowed deeply, but moved on without another word. Alison's eyes followed him even as she curtsied to a plump matron who reminded her of Aunt Cleo. Kilmore was dressed in the standard black swallow-tail coat, white shirt with starched white cravat, black skintight inexpressibles. Even his waistcoat was nothing out of the ordinary, a modest grey-and-brown striped silk. Yet he wore the ensemble with a dashing air that made him stand out in the crowd.

She hoped, very much, that he would ask her to dance.

Lord Fane was before her, the light of displeasure in his eyes as he noted the colour of her roses.

"I had hoped, Miss Larkin, that you might wear my flowers." His voice was stiff.

"Would that I might have done so, my lord. These were given me by Lord Edgehill, and Lady Emma advised me to carry them."

He was mollified. "Very proper. Perhaps you will be so kind as to grant me the second set, as well as the supper dance?"

"I shall look forward to it, sir."

There was a pause in the flow of arrivals, and Lady Emma was in consultation with her parents. As Lord Fane moved towards the ballroom, she turned to Alison.

"Mama and I must wait here a little longer, but Papa will take you in now to start the dancing. Off you go and enjoy yourself. Oh, one thing I nearly forgot—remember you must not stand up for the waltzes."

A group of guests was advancing on them and Lord Edgehill led her off before she could protest. She was not to waltz? But Philip had engaged her for the waltz. As she took her place with the earl at the head of the first set, as she went through the figures of the cotillion, she wondered what to do.

She had been anticipating with great pleasure waltzing with Philip again. He was a very proper gentleman; surely he would not have asked her if it was truly a terrible thing to do. Perhaps Lady Emma was being overcautious.

By the time Lord Edgehill handed her to Lord Fane, Alison had resolved to stand up for the waltz with Mr. Trevelyan whatever the consequences.

The country dance with Lord Fane left her with leisure to look about her. She spotted Philip dancing with a redheaded young lady—well, she did not wish to be uncharitable, but really, the poor girl's hair was positively carroty. She saw Lord Kilmore, who appeared to be watching her as he stood at the side of the room chatting to another gentleman. He even made a slight inclination of the head in her direction. She felt a hint of warmth in her cheeks and looked away.

Lady Emma was in the set next to hers, partnered by her older brother, Lord Gilchrist, whom Alison had met once. Fanny was a little farther down with a gentleman Alison did not know. She exchanged a quick smile with her friend as Lord Fane offered his arm for the promenade.

The dance over, his lordship led her to Lady Edgehill's side, as Lady Emma was at the far end of the room. Robert Gilchrist, in perfectly normal evening dress, was standing beside his mother. Alison had not seen him since the disastrous occasion of the poetry reading, and was not sure whether she had been forgiven.

He greeted her without apparent resentment. "My dance next, I collect, Miss Larkin."

Surprised, she looked at her card, which she had not yet had occasion to peruse. Mr. Gilchrist's name was written there in a hand suspiciously like his sister Emma's.

"A family precaution," the countess put in, "though in your case, my dear, quite unnecessary, I feel sure."

"Thank you, my lady," Alison said. "But are you sure you do not mind, sir? I owe you an apology, I fear, since the last time we met."

"Think nothing of it, ma'am. That wretched sonnet did need polishing. Luttrell warned me the particular line that set you off would not do for romantic poetry."

"Have you polished it?" she asked eagerly.

"Lord no, I'm not dabbling in verse any longer. As a matter of fact, I've taken up the flute. Splendid instrument, it is."

Disappointed to have lost her chance of a poem in her honour, Alison listened indulgently to his exposition of the wonders of music.

"Dashed if it ain't a good thing you laughed at me," he told her as he led her onto the floor. "Otherwise Bella might not have taken it into her head to play that evening and I never would have discovered that music is my true vocation."

Mr. Gilchrist was about the same age as Lord Fane, but his boyish enthusiasm made him seem much younger. Alison enjoyed dancing with him.

He was escorting her back to his mother when a lilting voice brought him to a halt. "Bob, me old friend, be a good fellow and introduce me to the lady."

Alison turned, and found herself staring into a pair of laughing eyes as blue as her own.

CHAPTER NINE

"NEIL, YOU DID COME after all!" Mr. Gilchrist appeared pleased. "Miss Larkin, allow me to present my friend Lord Deverill."

Alison felt as if she were looking into a sort of peculiar distorting mirror. Besides the merry blue eyes, the tall, slim young gentleman bowing over her hand had curly hair and features only sufficiently different from her own to make his face distinctly masculine.

Deverill had been her mother's maiden name.

"How do you do, my lord," she said faintly, wondering if it would be a horrid *faux pas* to enquire into the relationship.

"Sure and you must be a relative, Miss Larkin." Lord Deverill was frankly staring. "If you aren't the spit and image of me sister Eileen!"

"Are you by any chance Viscount Deverill of Ballycarrick, sir? Then I believe we must be cousins."

"The prettiest colleen in the room and she's me own cousin," marvelled his lordship with an engaging grin.

Mr. Gilchrist was looking from one to the other in amazement. "Dashed if you ain't like as two peas," he said. "I wonder that I never noticed it. I told you you'd enjoy my mother's ball, Neil, even if you ain't in the petticoat line. Coming to the card room?"

"What and leave me long lost relation? Never a bit, me boyo. You'll stand up with me for the next dance, cousin?"

"Oh yes, please! At least, I expect you ought to ask Lady Emma." She looked around but her chaperon was nowhere near.

"That's all right," Mr. Gilchrist assured her, "since he's a relative. I'll tell Emma."

As she and Lord Deverill joined a set, Alison was aware that they were attracting curious glances. The resemblance must be obvious and soon everyone would know that she had a cousin who was a viscount.

She quickly forgot that pleasure in the enjoyment of his company. They talked and laughed, somehow managing to keep their places in the dance with an occasional hint from the others in the set. Cousin Neil, as he asked her to call him, had a lively gaiety that perfectly complemented her own spirits. By the time the dance ended she felt she had known him for years.

"I must make you known to Lady Emma," she said firmly, tugging at his arm as they made their way off the floor. "I believe I saw her over by the orchestra."

"Have mercy, Cousin Alison, don't be thrusting me head into your dragon's mouth."

"She is not a dragon. She is young and pretty and excessively amiable. Besides, I must go to her and you cannot abandon me here."

He heaved an exaggerated sigh and followed meekly.

Alison became aware that Lord Kilmore was watching her again, his dark eyes enigmatic. He intrigued her. He had had no opportunity to approach her so far that evening, but doubtless now that she was going to sit with Lady Emma he would come and ask her to stand up with him.

She was not at all intrigued to see that Ralph Osborne was seated beside her chaperon. Annoyance more aptly described what she felt. The wretched man did not need to keep an eye on her for Aunt Zenobia while she was in a respectable ballroom! However, Mr. Osborne did not appear to have the least desire to keep an eye on her. He was deep in conversation with Lady Emma and neither of them looked up as she and Cousin Neil approached.

Robert Gilchrist was waiting there for his friend. Alison was about to greet him when she saw Fanny Witherington nearby, her partner having just left her with Lady Witherington. Fanny caught her eye, exchanged a word with her mother and came to join them.

Alison performed the necessary introductions, and Mr. Gilchrist promptly asked Fanny to dance. Alison recognized the light in his eye—just so had he looked when in the first throes of his sonnet. No doubt he would want to play his flute to Fanny.

Miss Witherington was consulting her card. "I am sorry, sir," she said with an apologetic smile, "but the next dance is a waltz. I have not yet received permission to waltz."

"Then the one after," persisted Mr. Gilchrist. "I shall go and ask your mama at once."

"Shall we sit out the waltz together?" Fanny asked Alison.

"Would it be really shocking to stand up?"

"Oh yes! Until you have been approved by one of the patronesses of Almack's it is enough to sink you forever."

Alison wondered how she was going to tell Mr. Trevelyan she was not going to dance with him. He was coming now, accompanied by the plump, almost dowdy lady who had reminded her of Aunt Cleo, but whose name she had not caught in the receiving line.

His smile was almost mischievous. "Lady Castlereagh, allow me to make Miss Larkin known to you."

Alison curtsied very low. Lady Castlereagh, wife of the Foreign Secretary and a patroness of Almack's, nodded to her good-naturedly.

"Philip has persuaded me to recommend him to you as a desirable partner for the waltz, Miss Larkin."

"Thank you, my lady, I shall be delighted." She should have known Philip had everything under control. Greatly daring, she added, "If you do not object, ma'am, I should like to present my friend and my cousin."

Her ladyship graciously consented. Miss Witherington and Lord Deverill, who had stepped back, were introduced. Philip, with an astonished look that made Alison want to giggle, shook hands with Cousin Neil.

"I expect you wish to stand up with Miss Witherington for the waltz, eh?" Lady Castlereagh said to Neil Deverill, just as Robert Gilchrist came back from speaking to Lady Witherington.

Robert glared at Neil.

"I should be honoured, ma'am," Neil said, with dancing imps in his blue eyes, "but I believe Mr. Gilchrist has the prior claim."

"Gilchrist? Edgehill's boy? Ah yes. Miss Witherington, I daresay you will like to waltz with Mr. Gilchrist." Beaming benevolently, her ladyship moved on.

"Save the next waltz for me, cousin," Neil murmured as Alison took Mr. Trevelyan's arm.

"So you have discovered a cousin," he said as he led her onto the floor.

"Is it not delightful? Mr. Gilchrist introduced us, though he had not the least notion we were related. Cousin Neil is beyond anything agreeable. You cannot know how much it means to me to have a relative who is both amiable and respectable."

"I believe I can guess." He was looking down at her with deep sympathy in his brown eyes. "What a valiant soul you are, Alison."

He swept her into the dance. As she circled the room in his arms, Alison was convinced that the world was perfect and that no one in it had ever been happier than she was at that moment.

When Philip escorted her back to Lady Emma, Lord Fane had taken Ralph Osborne's place. The evening had passed so quickly Alison had not realized that it was already time for the supper dance. Philip disappeared momentarily and returned with Lord Deverill in tow, whom he introduced to Lady Emma and Lord Fane as Robert Gilchrist's friend and Alison's cousin.

"You are a friend of Robert's?" Lady Emma queried. "And my wretched brother never noted the resemblance until you were face to face with Alison? We shall be happy to see you in Park Street at any time, Lord Deverill."

"Thank you, ma'am, I shall take advantage of your invitation. May I have the pleasure of this dance?" He cast a wickedly sparkling glance at Alison, daring her to remember how he had referred to her chaperon as a dragon.

Lady Emma shook her head. "Thank you, but I am promised to Mr. Trevelyan for supper. Here comes Robert, perhaps you can steal his partner."

Neil went off with Fanny Witherington to seek her mother's approval, leaving Mr. Gilchrist glowering after them. His sister's meaningful cough drew his attention back to present company.

"Your friend is charming," he said to Alison. "I daresay you know she plays the pianoforte, but perhaps she has not told you that her brother plays the flute? She has some music books for piano and flute with her in Town."

"How very fortunate!" said Alison, avoiding Mr. Trevelyan's eye. She knew very well he was thinking of the sonnet written to her eyes by the fickle young man.

"Miss Witherington is a pleasant young lady," Lord Fane put in. "I imagine you will attend her ball tomorrow, Miss Larkin? May I engage you in advance for the first dance?"

This time, even as she answered his lordship, she did meet Philip's eye. They could both see that Robert Gilchrist was frantically searching his memory to see if he had received an invitation to Fanny Witherington's ball. Only Lord Fane's sober presence stopped Alison from going into whoops.

The dance began. Alison and Lord Fane were near the bottom of the set and at first were at leisure to converse.

"I was glad to meet your cousin," he told her, "though I fear he may be a trifle rackety. Still, I was beginning to think you had no near relations, ha ha."

Alison was tempted to tell him that she had lots of relations no farther away than Great Ormond Street, but she held her tongue and smiled sweetly. His description of Neil as rackety she dismissed. Her cousin was a dear, and she would not hear anything against him. Lord Fane had used the same word of Lord Kilmore, so he probably considered all gentlemen rackety who had not his own serious, responsible character.

They were joined at supper by Cousin Neil and Fanny, with Robert Gilchrist hanging on as a determined third, and Lady Emma and Philip Trevelyan. Lord Fane solicitously plied Alison with such delicacies as salmon in aspic and apricot gateaux. She scarcely noticed what she was eating, as she was far more interested in watching Neil tease Robert by flirting with Fanny.

Miss Witherington was master of the entire repertoire of coy glances, artful turns of the fan, slyly innocent rejoinders. It was an education to Alison, who had never flirted with anyone. It looked like fun, but whom was she to try it on?

Philip was her friend, Neil was her cousin, Robert had one of his instant tendres for Fanny and Lord Fane was unlikely to appreciate such dashing behaviour. At that fortuitous moment her glance fell on Lord Kilmore at the next table. He smiled at her, a faintly mocking smile. If he ever asked her to dance, he might prove to be the very person to enjoy a mild flirtation.

Robert was beginning to look sulky.

Fanny apparently realized she had gone far enough if she wanted to retain his interest. Turning to Alison, she said, "I have been meaning to tell you, Mr. Gilchrist happened to mention that he plays the flute. It is of all instruments the most delightful. My brother plays and I have some of his music with me—is it not a lucky chance?"

"Most fortunate," Alison agreed gravely, all too aware that Lady Emma and Mr. Trevelyan were exchanging amused glances.

"Miss Witherington has kindly offered to accompany me," said Mr. Gilchrist in a grand manner, then added with a touch of anxiety, "She says she has some easy pieces, folk songs and such."

"Irish folk songs," said Fanny, laughing. "Lord Deverill, do you sing?"

"Faith and what Irishman does not know the songs of Ireland?" Neil's blue eyes were twinkling, but he soothed his scowling friend by adding, "I'll be happy to join you both if Cousin Alison will lend her sweet voice in support."

Lady Emma nodded, so Alison assented. She could not read music, but with Neil and Fanny to help she would manage. Robert, realizing that in any case a chaperon would be needed, abandoned his chagrin and a date was set.

Lord Fane looked disgruntled at his exclusion. "I hope you mean to give us a concert when you have practiced," he said, putting a good face on it. "I fear I have no musical ability, but I am a talented audience."

Alison rewarded his joke with a laugh. She was relieved, however, when later on Lady Emma whispered to her, "A little competition, real or imagined, will do Lord Fane no harm. You must not let him take you for granted."

Neither Alison nor Fanny sat out a single dance for the rest of the night. It was nearly dawn by the time the landau deposited Lady Emma and her protégée at the house in Park Street. Alison wanted to discuss the joys of her first ball, and to ask advice on one of many perplexities.

"Not now, you unnatural child," groaned Lady Emma. "We have another ball tonight, remember. I, at least, need some sleep!"

So Alison retired to bed to ponder the puzzling question of why Lord Kilmore had watched her all night without ever making the least attempt even to speak to her.

CHAPTER TEN

IT DID NOT SEEM POSSIBLE that Alison could enjoy Fanny's ball even more than her own, but she did. There were two reasons for this. First of all, she no longer felt herself the cynosure of all eyes. In the second place, Lord Kilmore at last asked her to stand up with him.

"Why did you keep gazing at me last night, my lord?" she asked as soon as they took their places.

"You are not one to mince words, are you, Miss Larkin?" His smile held the mockery she remembered. "My intention was to tantalize you. Did I succeed?"

She glanced up at him through lowered lashes, experimenting with the way she had seen Fanny do it.

"La, sir, I did not even notice, I vow."

He laughed, with genuine amusement. "Coming it altogether too strong, my dear. I watched you because I was afraid that if I took my eyes off you for an instant you would vanish like some forest sprite. That is what you looked like, all silver and white amid the rustic greenery."

"Oh no, sir, I am made of flesh and blood." She hoped her eyes were round and innocent.

His gaze grew warm and he pulled her a little closer. "I am aware of that."

That had been the wrong thing to say, Alison realized. This flirting business was more complicated than it appeared. With considerable relief she pointed out, "It is our turn to lead."

When they again had leisure to converse, the mockery was back in his expression. "Do you not want to know why I did not ask you to dance last night, Miss Larkin?" he enquired.

She eyed him with speculative caution. Curiosity won. "Tell me."

"I was afraid I might be called out if I dispossessed any of your partners."

"You mean a duel? Then you think my partners tonight are less likely to challenge you? That is unhandsome of you, sir."

"On the contrary, ma'am, when I saw you tonight I knew I was ready to risk my life for the bliss of one moment at your side."

"And has that moment lived up to your expectation, my lord?" Alison ventured archly.

"What if I should say it has not?"

"Then perhaps I shall challenge you myself."

His shout of laughter made everyone stare. "I believe you might. Allow me to assure you that my every expectation has been exceeded. And your talent at the art of flirtation progresses rapidly with practice."

"I have a good teacher, sir."

"Saucy wench. Your dimples are adorable. It is our turn to lead, I believe, ma'am."

Once again, Alison was glad of a respite. Lord Kilmore was constantly taking her by surprise. He was fascinating but, she had to admit, a bit disconcerting.

She looked forward to her next dance, a waltz with Philip, when she could relax and be herself.

Philip was also looking forward to the waltz. He wanted to know what Kilmore was saying that made Alison's eyes sparkle so, and he had no doubt but that she would tell him. Her artless confidences were a delight, her trust in him a pleasure of a deeper sort. He found it hard to believe that he had ever thought her a vulgar hussy.

Her enjoyment of her success was whole-hearted and innocent. For Emma's sake he would make sure nothing happened to mar Alison's happiness. He was even willing to aid and abet her intention of marrying a lord.

"So you have added another lord to your string," he greeted her.

She laughed. "Lord Kilmore? He is a wicked flirt."

"What has he been saying to you?"

"A dozen things, none of them worth repeating. Some of them excessively silly, in fact. You know, I used to suppose that all lords were alike. At least Mrs. Meeke and Mrs. Cuthbertson would have it so. I am quite undeceived. Lord Kilmore is a flirt, and Lord Fane is gallant and respectable, and Cousin Neil is a merry dear, and Lord Edgehill is, well, elderly."

"Four!"

"I have danced with two others, whose names I have forgot." She looked absurdly guilty.

"That makes six. A goodly total. Which do you like best?"

The music began while she was considering, and she moved into Philip's arms as if she felt she belonged there. Her hand on his shoulder, feather-light, sent an inexplicable *frisson* racing through his body. He had to concentrate to follow her words.

"I like them all, in different ways. Cousin Neil best, perhaps, because he is a relative."

"You have a laudable sense of family loyalty."

"My family is worth being loyal to. Lady Emma told me you are close to your brothers and sisters."

"Yes, my family is dear to me." He found himself talking about his sisters, their husbands and children. "But you cannot be interested in strangers."

"I am," Alison assured him earnestly. "They are not quite strangers, for they are all part of you."

So he went on to tell her of his clergyman brother, recently engaged to be married, and his naval brother who was expecting a promotion to captain of his own ship. She peppered him with questions. Scarcely noticing that the waltz had finished, they continued to walk around the room together until an indignant Robert Gilchrist confronted them.

"Dash it, Miss Larkin, I've been looking for you all over the place. If you mean to dance with me, we had best join a set before it is too late."

Philip hurriedly apologized and went to find his next partner. He had not danced so much in years, but he did not want the tattlemongers to be able to say that he only stood up with Lady Emma and her protégée.

That did not stop him waltzing with Emma later that night. She was a graceful dancer and they moved together well, but somehow her calm self-sufficiency was less satisfying than usual. The memory of Alison's lively enthusiasm and sparkling eyes came between them.

"You are to be congratulated on Miss Larkin's success," he said. "You have done wonders with her."

"She is a charming child. I do not wonder that the gentlemen flock about her, though doubtless the rumours of her fortune are no hindrance to her popularity. Mr. Osborne is concerned lest she be taken in by some ne'er-do-well fortune hunter.''

"I saw you talking to him at your ball last night." Philip wondered if he was imagining the touch of pink in her cheeks.

"Yes, I thought he ought to be there so as to be able to report to Mrs. Winkle. He is very gentlemanly, do you not think? I don't believe anyone would guess him to be an India merchant.''

"I doubt anyone cast a second glance.''

"I promised to try to obtain some invitations for him. Just so that he can keep an eye on Alison," she added quickly.

"Of course. I'll see what I can do to help.''

"Thank you, Philip, I can always rely on you. To satisfy Mrs. Winkle must be my first concern. I expect she will be *aux anges* at Lord Deverill's acceptance of Alison as a close relative. Alison herself is in raptures.'' Emma chuckled. "Did you hear her ordering him to ask that unhappy beanpole with the teeth for a dance?''

"She is kind. I have no doubt that she will soon have as many female friends as male admirers. Miss Witherington seems devoted to her already.''

"Yes, she and Fanny are bosom bows. A most fortunate acquaintance. She *is* a success, is she not?''

OVER THE NEXT MONTH Alison's success showed no signs of diminishing. Philip attended many of the same events, routs and breakfasts, dinners, soirées and balls. He was present when she made her triumphal appearance at Almack's, thanks to his introduction to Lady Castlereagh, and he was the recipient of her whispered declaration that the refreshments were even worse than she had expected. At every entertainment where there was dancing he engaged her in advance for a single waltz.

In fact, the one time he was tardy in asking her, she reminded him. He was not sure whether waltzing with him had become a habit to her, or whether she looked forward to their dances as much as he did.

While she never lacked for partners, the group of particular friends who surrounded her on most occasions remained the same. Fanny Witherington was always there, as was Robert Gilchrist. At first Philip thought young Robert was surprisingly compliant with his sister's request for an escort for her protégée. It soon became plain that Fanny was the attraction.

Lord Fane and Lord Deverill were both steadfast in their attentions to Alison. Philip was privileged to hear their opinions of each other.

"The man's a pompous ass," Neil Deverill grumbled to him. "I'm damned if I know what Alison sees in him."

"Solid worth," Philip suggested.

Deverill snorted with laughter. "Solid's the right word. Faith, he'll be a tub of lard by the time he's forty."

Philip could not help liking Alison's cousin, nor could he help suspecting that Lord Fane's view was correct: "The man's a damned here-and-thereian. These Irish titles are all the same: no solid worth to them."

"He's something of a scapegrace," Philip admitted, hiding his amusement at hearing his own words on Fane's lips. "There's no harm in him, though, I believe."

"It's a pity Miss Larkin has no more respectable relations in Town, but she cannot be blamed for that. I shall make it my business to see that Deverill does no harm to her reputation."

Philip was more concerned about Lord Kilmore's less conspicuous attentions. The baron was not a constant member of the group around Alison, but when he was present at a ball he invariably stood up with her twice. It was obvious that she found him fascinating. Chiding himself for a busybody, Philip noticed that she behaved quite differently with Kilmore than with anyone else. His consolation was that she had told him she considered his lordship a shocking flirt.

Kilmore's reputation was not precisely unsavoury, but he was something of a rake, and the fact that he lived on the edge of Dun Territory was common knowledge.

To be sure, Mrs. Winkle's fortune was sufficient to support an expensive spendthrift. Philip had come to know Ralph Osborne better in the past few weeks; he was sure the man knew how to tie up that fortune so that no extravagant husband could leave Alison going home by beggar's bush. If Alison fell in love with Kilmore, there was no logical reason why she should not marry him.

There was only Philip's heart telling him that she would never be happy with a rake. She would be better off with that "pompous ass," Fane, who showed signs of being perturbed by Kilmore's pursuit of the object of his affection.

Philip debated whether to warn Alison, or at least Emma. But Emma knew Kilmore's reputation. She would wonder at his unnecessary interference. He said nothing.

Neither Lord Fane nor Lord Kilmore was present at Lady Witherington's musicale. Philip would not have missed the occasion for the world. He sat patiently through harpsichord sonatas and harp suites and Italian arias, for the most part more notable for *brio* than *grazia*. He quite understood why Neil Deverill had refused to turn up at the beginning of the evening.

Seated beside him, Alison fidgeted and kept peering over her shoulder. "They are all so *good,*" she moaned as a plump soprano in pink curtsied, beaming and breathless. "If Neil does not come I cannot do it. I simply cannot hold a note without him singing, too."

"He will come," Philip soothed, taking her restless hand in his and patting it in what he hoped was an avuncular manner.

"I am glad Lord Fane could not come tonight, to see me making a cake of myself."

"He would have noticed only that you are quite the prettiest performer in the room."

She looked up at him in surprise, for he was not given to compliments. For a heart-stopping moment their gazes held; the wild roses in her cheeks took on a deeper hue. Then the absentee slid into the chair on her other side and she turned to him in joyful greeting.

"Neil! I was afraid you would come too late, you odious creature."

"Faith, cousin, I'd not let you down before yon Sassenachs."

"Hush!" someone hissed behind them as a tall, thin girl ran her fingers across her harp.

"Sure and she could climb right through her own instrument," whispered the irrepressible viscount.

The harpist finished and it was time for the grand finale. Footmen pushed the pianoforte to the centre of the dais as Fanny and Robert made their way to the front, the latter carrying his flute and looking decidedly self-conscious.

"I can't!" said Alison, looking from Neil to Philip in sudden panic.

"You can," they chorused, and Emma nodded encouragement from Philip's other side. Neil took her hands and hauled her to her feet, then led her up to the dais, one arm about her shoulders, whispering in her ear.

Philip noted that he kept her hand in his as they turned to face the audience. For support, of course; they could be brother and sister. They were a handsome pair, Alison in a simple gown of palest blue, Deverill with a blue satin waistcoat under his black coat. Was the coat a trifle shiny at the elbows? Philip told himself to stop looking for flaws.

The performance was delightful. Alison's voice was not strong, but in unison with her cousin she sang true, enjoying herself whole-heartedly after her nervous start. A haunting Irish air was followed by a jig for flute and piano alone, and then a ballad. There were cries of encore and they finished with another air, to vigorous applause.

Grinning exultantly, Neil picked Alison up in a hug and swung her around. Philip frowned and turned to make some comment to Emma. She was watching her brother and Miss Witherington, who had their heads together over some music, apparently oblivious of the audience's enthusiastic reception.

"Do you know," Emma observed, "it would not surprise me if Robert and Fanny were to make a match of it. Robert has never before admired the same female for more than a fortnight, and Mama says he practises the flute for hours at a time until she is driven to distraction."

"At least poetry was silent."

"Not the way Robert did it. He was used to wander about trying out phrases in a semiaudible mutter. But I am serious. He seems to be growing up at last. At least, he no longer falls into the sulks at the slightest thing."

"That is hardly sufficient basis for a marriage!"

"No, you are right. I go too fast. But it would be an unexceptionable connexion on both sides. I am sure Papa and Mama would happily give their consent."

"Wait until Robert offers, my dear," Philip advised her. He wanted to ask whether a match between Alison and her cousin would be equally acceptable to all concerned, but people were approaching to congratulate Emma on her protégée's performance. Alison, eyes bright, face flushed, appeared at his side dragging Deverill after her.

"What did you think?" she asked, and he had to assure her that the Irish had won the day.

Within a few days, his unvoiced question about Neil's acceptability was unexpectedly answered. With some reluctance he had agreed to accompany a friend on an expedition to retrieve an imprudent younger brother from one of the more notorious gambling houses of the city.

Number Seventy-Seven St. James's Street, for all its fashionable address, had relieved as many young bucks of their fortunes as any less elegant hell. The bruiser who admitted them was clad in bulging evening dress, but his broken nose and cauliflower ear proclaimed him a veteran of the ring. Assaulted by stale fumes of wine and tobacco, Philip's nostrils wrinkled as he stepped into the main saloon. Beneath chandeliers and hangings fit to grace any ballroom, a noisy throng of well-born gamesters and high-flying Cyprians crowded around the tables. Not a few were underneath.

Philip was not pleased to see Lord Deverill seated at the roulette table, his avid gaze on the bouncing ball as it rattled around the wheel.

As Philip watched, the ball settled in a slot. Deverill sighed, pushed back his chair and stood up. Philip abandoned his friend without a second thought.

"Lost much?"

"What?" The viscount turned, startled by the quiet voice at his ear. "Oh...no." He grinned. "I didn't have much to lose. Sure and I don't mind admitting, Mr. Trevelyan, that it's low tide with me. I ought to stay away from the tables. I've better luck on the horses."

Philip's immediate impulse was to offer the man a couple of hundred pounds—he'd even go as high as a monkey—to take himself back to Ireland and stay out of Alison's life. He looked at the candid, rueful face, the blue eyes and black curls so like hers, and changed his mind. At least he was not the worse for drink. Alison was prodigious fond of her rapscallion cousin, and whatever his faults he lent her consequence by his very existence. A word to Emma would be sufficient to ensure that matters went no further.

"Perhaps this will tide you over," he said, extracting a twenty pound note from a roll of flimsies. He did not for a moment believe Deverill's promise of prompt repayment.

His friend reappeared at that moment with a hangdog youth in his grasp. They headed for the exit.

Philip called on Emma the following afternoon. Alison was driving in the Park with Lord Fane, so he was able to pass on his warning without roundaboutation.

"So it seems the fellow is a penniless adventurer," he finished. "You will know best how to tell Al...Miss Larkin."

"Yes, it will not do for her to develop a tendre in that direction," Emma murmured. "It is already bad enough that he is a first cousin. I shall see that she understands the situation. Oh dear, she does hold him in considerable affection. I hope she will not be out-of-reason distressed."

Emma seemed somewhat distraite so Philip did not stay long. As he was walking homeward along Park Street, enjoying the fine April day, he saw Ralph Osborne coming towards him. Doubtless Emma would inform Mrs. Winkle's watchdog of Lord Deverill's pecuniary embarrassment. Another vigilant pair of eyes would be fixed on the poor fellow at every turn and Alison's safety, if not her happiness, was assured.

He felt a pang of regret as he exchanged brief greetings with Mr. Osborne and walked on.

CHAPTER ELEVEN

REGRET WAS Alison's first emotion when Lady Emma told her that Lord Deverill had nary a feather to fly with.

"If only I had known!" she exclaimed. "How shocking that my own cousin should be in need when I have so much of everything. Do you think he will be offended if I offer to help? There must be some tactful way to do it."

"I hardly think your aunt will permit you to support the viscount with her money."

Her face fell. "I had not thought. I daresay my two pounds a week will not go very far for a gentleman."

"My dear, anything you give him will immediately vanish on the gaming tables. I did not want to tell you, but Philip met him in a gambling club."

"But all gentlemen gamble. That does not mean Neil's pockets are to let. Phil...Mr. Trevelyan himself was at the club, you just said so."

"Though I cannot deny that most gentlemen gamble, Philip was there with a friend for quite another purpose. Nor is he guessing about the state of Deverill's pockets. It seems your cousin admitted that he is purse-pinched."

"There must be something I can do to help him!"

Lady Emma shrugged. "I doubt he will starve. He is a personable young man and a favourite with hostesses. As a peer, he cannot be imprisoned for debt."

"If there is nothing I can do, why did Mr. Trevelyan tell you?"

"He wanted me to put you on your guard. I have told you that any young woman with your expectations is bound to be a target for fortune hunters."

"Cousin Neil is not a... You mean he wants to marry me for my money?" Alison's forehead wrinkled. "I do not believe that he wants to marry me at all. He is like a brother to me."

"Don't frown, you will develop lines," said Lady Emma automatically. "I would not go so far as to say that Deverill has designs upon your fortune, but it is best that you should be aware of the possibility. While we are on the subject, I ought to warn you that Lord Kilmore, too, is said to be badly dipped, and his reputation in other matters is far from spotless."

"Lord Kilmore!" Surprise turned to thoughtfulness. "You know, I can imagine that he might marry for money. I can never be sure what is going on in his head. If you think it best, I shall try to be stand-offish with him, but indeed I cannot cut poor Neil."

"I shall not ask it of you, my dear. On the whole, he is an asset to you."

Alison sighed. "That is two lords who are ineligible. The real world is not at all like Mrs. Cuthbertson's novels. Lord Fane *is* as respectable as he appears, is he not?" she added anxiously.

"Thoroughly respectable, and more and more enamoured, if I am any judge. I beg you will not count on his declaring himself though, Alison. Sooner or later he must discover the other side of your family, and whether his admiration for you is strong enough to overcome that disadvantage I cannot guess.''

''I do not like to deceive him. Perhaps it is best that he should find out soon.''

''Pray do not do anything precipitate. It takes time to build a solid foundation of attachment that will not be rocked by the disclosure of your father's birth.''

Alison was not convinced. Besides her dislike of deceit and of acting as if she was ashamed of her family, she hated the uncertainty. How dreadful it would be if she came to love Lord Fane, only to have him turn tail after she had given him her heart.

She had to admit that so far that organ had remained remarkably untouched by the gentleman's undoubted virtues.

Two days later, not having seen Lord Fane in the interim, she received an invitation from him. She was at breakfast with Lady Emma, and Philip had joined them for a cup of coffee as he sometimes did after an early ride in the Park.

''This is for you, Alison.'' Lady Emma passed her a sheet of paper from the pile of post beside her plate. ''Though very properly addressed to me.''

''From one of your admirers, then.'' Philip smiled at her. He was excessively handsome in his well-fitted riding clothes. His usually immaculate hair was slightly ruffled and the exercise had brought colour to his cheeks.

Alison scanned the brief letter. ''It is from Lord Fane. He has been called out of Town for a few days, but before he left he procured a box at Drury Lane for . . . Oh, the play is *Antony and Cleopatra!* And he asks us to make up a party for him, ma'am, if we care to go, as he will return only just in time for the performance. How Aunt Cleo would love to see it."

"Out of the question," said Lady Emma at once.

Alison turned to Mr. Trevelyan with a pleading look.

"Emma is right, I'm afraid. It simply will not do."

Alison's shoulders slumped but she tried to keep the disappointment from her voice as she said, "Then will you join us, sir?"

"As a matter of fact I have my own box, but alas! I am behindhand with my invitation to you."

"We could pretend you asked us first," Alison suggested hopefully. "Lord Fane would never know."

"I have a better idea. Think you that your aunts would honour me with their company?"

"Oh, sir!" Pushing back her chair she ran around the table to drop a kiss on his cheek. She started back at once, crimson-faced and appalled at her own impulsive action. "I . . . I beg your pardon," she stammered. "I did not mean to . . ."

"Why, I rather hoped that you did." His face was equally red, but a warm light in his eyes belied his mocking tone. "No gentleman with the least degree of sensibility can object to being kissed by a pretty young lady. I take it you approve of my notion?"

"Did you mean it? You will invite all my aunts to the theatre? Oh sir."

"Not again!" said Lady Emma hastily, holding up her hand. "Really, Alison, I cannot think what came over you. If it had been anyone but Philip we should have had a full-blown scandal on our hands."

"I'm very sorry, ma'am. But only Mr. Trevelyan would have made such a suggestion, so there was not the least danger."

Philip laughed. "I'm glad to hear it," he said, standing up. "I must be off to pen a note of invitation. Emma, will you drive with me this afternoon?"

"I'm sorry, I am expecting a visitor." Her cheeks were pink now, too, Alison noted in surprise. It must be catching.

"Then will you be so kind as to join me, Miss Alison?"

She curtsied and said in her primmest voice, "Thank you, sir, I shall be delighted."

He bowed deeply over her hand and she half expected a formal retort to match hers. All he said was, "Minx!" and took his leave.

Alison sat down again to finish her buttered eggs. Lady Emma did not give her the scolding she knew she deserved. Her chaperon sipped her tea from a delicate Crown Derby cup while regarding one of her letters with a dreamy smile. It was most unlike the practical Lady Emma.

"I must return a book to Hookham's this morning, ma'am," Alison regretfully interrupted her reverie. "Is there any errand I can do for you?"

"What? Oh yes, if you would not mind picking up the fan I left to be mended. Be sure to take Carter or Henry."

Now Alison knew that Lady Emma was lost in an airdream. It was weeks since she had needed to be reminded to take a servant with her when she went out.

"If you will tell me whom you wish to ask to join us in Lord Fane's box," Alison persisted, "I shall save you the trouble of writing invitations."

"Box?"

"At Drury Lane."

"Ah yes. Fanny and Robert will do."

"And another gentleman, since Mr. Trevelyan has his own box?"

"Do you think Mr. Osborne would enjoy the play?"

Alison frowned. Was she to be watched over even at the theatre? Then she had an idea. "I do not know if he likes Shakespeare, but if he comes he can take me to Mr. Trevelyan's box to see my aunts, and no one else need be the wiser. That is a splendid notion. I shall write to him at once."

Her chores completed, Alison dressed to go driving. She put on a new primrose promenade dress with lilac ribbons and a matching lilac spencer. Her straw hat had silk lilac blossoms alternating with posies of primroses around the brim. White kid half-boots and gloves, and a white parasol with primrose ribbons completed the ensemble. She twirled before the mirror. If Philip had called her pretty this morning in her old morning gown, what would he say to her now?

She laughed softly to herself. Probably nothing, but she liked to look her best for him anyway.

In fact, his first words as he handed her into the tilbury had nothing to do with her appearance. "I sent a footman with my invitation to the Misses Larkin this morning, and one of your lads brought a response not half an hour ago. They would dearly love to accept, but it seems your Aunt Di is indisposed and may not be able to go."

"Aunt Di is ill? Please, will you take me there instead of the Park?"

"She wrote herself. I do not believe she is seriously ill. Would you not prefer to show off your dashing outfit to the Fashionable World?"

"Don't be caperwitted," she said severely. "I must go and make sure that Aunt Di is all right. Even if she is, I expect she cannot walk Midnight, and no one else can manage him. I shall have to take him out.''

Philip groaned. ''I'll call you a hackney,'' he offered.

For a moment she thought he was serious, but even as he spoke he gave Spaniard and Conqueror the office to start and turned their heads towards the unfashionable regions of the city.

He even walked with her and Midnight through the muddy fields around the brick kilns east of Grays Inn Lane. Though his glossy hessians were horridly splashed, he only murmured, regarding them thoughtfully, ''That will give my valet something to worry about for a change.''

Alison was not allowed to see Aunt Di, who had nothing worse than a bad cold and hoped to recover in time to see *Antony and Cleopatra*. By the third day her health was sufficiently improved to allow her to walk Midnight herself. Unfortunately, the cold had already been passed on to Aunt Cleo. It hit her much harder. By the day of the performance she was confined to her bed with a raging fever and a putrid sore throat.

Squeak brought a wavery note from Aunt Polly: Di was nursing Cleo and the household was all at sixes and sevens. What was she to do?

No argument of Lady Emma's served to persuade Alison that her duty lay anywhere but at her aunts' service, whatever Lord Fane might think of her defection.

''Indeed I shall be very sorry if his lordship is offended, ma'am, but I *must* go. Poor Aunt Polly is simply unable to manage, and I cannot forget how my aunts nursed me through all my childhood illnesses. You will make my excuses to Lord Fane?'' she pleaded.

"Of course, my dear, yet it is no good pretending that he will not be gravely displeased."

"I am very sorry for it," Alison repeated helplessly, "but I have no choice."

Within half an hour she had packed up the simplest of her new clothes, and Lady Emma's landau carried her back to her old home.

Philip found her there the next morning. She was in the kitchen, sitting at the table with Polly, a trio of ragamuffins and a scrawny child Philip assumed to be the scullery maid. A large tome was open on the table before Alison, who was poring with wrinkled forehead over the faded, spidery writing, liberally spotted with unidentifiable stains.

She looked up as he entered and her expression brightened. "Philip! Perhaps you can guess what this means. I want to make a Restorative Meat Jelly for Aunt Cleo but I cannot read the receipt. Move over, Squeak, and let the gentleman sit down."

The urchin kneeling on the chair beside her to squint at the book obligingly vacated his place. The four youngest members of the company were all staring at Philip with wide eyes.

"Us di'n't ought to be 'ere," said the boy with the freckles.

Aunt Polly found her voice. "Alison, dear, Mr. Trevelyan should be entertained in the parlour," she pointed out timidly.

"Your maid very properly tried to show me in there," he assured her. "I am the intruder here and should not dream of turning anyone else out. Let me see that, Miss Alison." He had noted her slip of the tongue in addressing him by his Christian name, but this was no time to tease her about it.

She pushed the book closer to him and their heads bent together over the besmirched pages. "The bits I can read are rather horrid. This says fresh killed Gravy Beef. I daresay the butcher will know what that is. And I'm afraid this must be one Calf's Foot. But there is a spot right on top of this word and none of us can guess what it says. '2 or 3 lb. *K* blank *eal*,' you see?"

"We ought to manage between us; we have proven our talent for word puzzles. Let me think. *K*—that suggests *kn* to me. *Nnn—eal*."

"Knuckle o' veal," piped up a timid voice. The scullery maid turned scarlet and hid her face in her apron.

"Bitsy, how clever of you!" Alison exclaimed. "That must be it."

"Why'd Miss Cleo write *K* if she meant *N?*" enquired the boy who had spoken before. "It don't make no sense."

"That's acos you're iggerent, Joe," Squeak said, his high voice managing to convey condescension. "*K* comes afore *N* in lots o' words. Knuckle an' knife an' knee an' such."

"Dub yer mummer or you'll get a taste o' my knuckles," Tarry Joe growled.

Philip glanced at Alison. Serenely ignoring the boys' squabble she was perusing the rest of the receipt, her little nose wrinkled in distaste.

"Oh dear, you have to skim off the scum as it cooks. With a spoon, I wonder?"

"Cease to wonder." Philip pulled the book away from her and closed it with a thump. "My chef has an excellent assistant who is quite capable of preparing a Restorative Meat Jelly and anything else you need. Lead me to pen and paper, and he shall be here within the hour. Tarry Joe, it was you, was it not, who delivered a message to my house the other day?"

"Us all knows where you lives, guv," Bubble informed him. "Us knows all the places—"

"Hush!" his brother and Tarry Joe admonished.

Philip was inclined to investigate this odd exchange, but Alison invited him to go with her to the drawing-room in search of writing materials and he let the matter drop.

Having written and dispatched the instructions to his chef, to send his assistant to take over the Larkins' kitchen, Philip was glad of a chance to speak privately with Alison. Polly had vanished in her silent way and except for Midnight, who had followed them from the kitchen, they were alone together in the green silk jungle.

The first thing he did was to point out this deplorable fact. "I trust your aunts do not make a practice of leaving you unchaperoned."

"You are the only gentleman who has ever visited me here. Shall I call Aunt Polly?"

"No, no! Midnight's presence will suffice this once." Hearing his name, the dog came to lay his heavy head on Philip's knee. He ran the coarse-furred black ears through his fingers as he spoke. "I wanted to tell you about the theatre last night."

"I am sorry to have missed the play, but I *could* not go while Aunt Cleo is ill."

"I know, and so I explained to Fane. He was, to say the least, put out by your absence, but I believe I succeeded in reinstating you in his favour. Unfortunately, I found it impossible not to tell him where you are. You may not long be able to say that I am your only gentleman-caller to this house."

Relief chased dismay across her expressive face. "You think he will come here? I own I shall be glad to have him know about my family, but I did not expect that he would actually visit Great Ormond Street."

"I'm sorry. It would have presented a very odd appearance had I refused to give your direction."

"You must not think that I hold you responsible. It was excessively kind in you to persuade him to forgive me for missing his party. But it is sadly beneath his dignity to come to this part of Town. How chivalrous he is!"

"Chivalrous indeed." Philip did not mention his suggestion that Fane would not care to visit a house of sickness. Fanny Witherington had promptly declared her intention of going to see her friend, whatever her mama might say. After that, his lordship's dignity was in more danger if he backed out than from calling in Great Ormond Street.

Alison did not appear to think that Philip's visit was a noteworthy demonstration of chivalry. However, on his departure she accompanied him into the hall, saying earnestly, "I do not know how to thank you for the loan of your cook, sir. It is the sort of generosity I have come to expect of you. The rest of us were satisfied with bread and cheese, but poor Aunt Cleo cannot swallow properly."

"Has a doctor seen her?"

"Yes, he came yesterday and again today. She is very ill." Alison pressed her lips together in an effort to hold back the tears that swam in her blue eyes.

Philip enfolded her in his arms. Clutching his lapel, she sobbed quietly for a minute against his chest, then he felt the effort she made to regain her composure.

"Bitsy," he said in a conversational tone, to help her. "I have it. Her real name is Betsy, but she is such a little bit of a thing..."

"You *are* good at riddles." With a watery smile, she raised her tear-stained face to smile at him.

He managed not to kiss her.

CHAPTER TWELVE

Aunt Cleo was soon pronounced out of danger, but she still required Aunt Di's constant attendance, and so Alison was needed to run the household. Aunt Polly had reached a *modus vivendi* with the gardener hired by Aunt Zenobia but simply could not manage the other servants.

Lord Fane visited twice, before announcing that he had urgent business on his estate and must leave Town for a week. Alison wondered whether she would ever see him again after this obvious excuse. His appalled fascination with the tiger hangings in the drawing-room, his uneasy condescension to Aunt Polly, who acted as chaperon, and to Aunt Di when she came down to make his acquaintance, made it plain that he was uncomfortable.

Alison had little leisure to ponder the possible loss of her only remaining eligible lord. She received a letter from Fanny bemoaning the fact that her mama would not let her risk her health, but she did not lack for visitors.

Cousin Neil called one afternoon, his gaiety cheering her. He considered the drawing-room hangings a huge joke. Unfortunately, he also found the aunts a source of amusement, though he politely refrained from laughing aloud in their presence. The fact that his own aunt had married into this family was exquisitely funny. Alison was quite cross with him, and glad that as he was a relative she did not need Aunt Polly as chaperon.

"If my father had not married my mother, he might have found a rich wife instead," she pointed out. "Then my aunts would have had a comfortable life instead of scraping for every penny."

"And you'd not have been born." He sobered. "Faith, 'tis a terrible thought. I beg your pardon, cousin, but I've had a spot of luck and the world is a bright place this day."

"Luck?" Not wanting to embarrass him, she had never told him she knew he was in the basket.

"A grand day at the races and I've come away with a pocketful of the ready. I even paid back Trevelyan."

"Neil, you never borrowed from Mr. Trevelyan!" She was dismayed.

"I never asked him for a penny, but I'd be a fool to turn down an offer, now wouldn't I?" He grinned. "By his face, I'd guess he'd not reckoned to see his blunt again. There's enough left to stake me to a big win."

"Could you not stop gambling, Neil, while you are ahead? You might lose it all again."

He shrugged. "'Tis a risk, of course, but until I have what I need I must go on trying. I'd not have you think me a hardened gambler, my dear. There's Bridey waiting for me in Ballycarrick to carry her off to a new life, and a new life takes money."

"Bridey? You have an Irish sweetheart?"

"Bridget McConigle, the sweetest lass that ever breathed the blessed air of Ireland."

"And she is waiting for you?"

"Her pa, old man McConigle, is a farmer, as cross-grained an old codger as you will ever see. He's no time for titles and he don't mean to let his only daughter wed an impoverished viscount." Neil explained that he wanted to emigrate with his beloved to Canada or America, but he needed the wherewithal to start out.

"I shall ask Aunt Zenobia to advance a part of my inheritance," Alison said at once. "Everyone keeps telling me she is rich as Croesus, so I can certainly spare enough to let you marry your Bridey."

"The devil you will!" He jumped up and moved restlessly about the room. Midnight watched him with suspicion. "I'm not asking for charity, Alison."

"But we are cousins!"

"Leave a man a little pride!" He smiled ruefully. "Winning a wager is one step above begging from relatives, I hope. Now tell me, are you sad to be missing the balls and parties?"

Recognizing his efforts to change the subject, Alison did not speak to him again of Bridey, though he continued to visit frequently.

Another visitor arrived when she was in the kitchen discussing with Mr. Trevelyan's cook a menu to tempt the appetite of a convalescent. The parlourmaid put her head round the door.

"Ge'mun to see you, miss. Lord Kilmore, he says." Bess was growing quite blasé about the stream of titled callers. "I put 'im in the drawing-room."

"Lord Kilmore!" Alison was even more astonished than when Lord Fane had been announced. A dashing buck to risk being seen in the wrong part of Town for her sake! It was very flattering, even if he was as ineligible as Cousin Neil. "Tell him I shall join him at once, Bess. Bitsy," she added to the scullery maid, "call Miss Polly, if you please."

She surprised the gentleman with an expression of disdain on his handsome face as he contemplated the silken jungle. He turned at her entrance and bowed gracefully, a quizzical look in his eyes.

"You live in interesting surroundings, Miss Larkin."

That made her laugh. "My aunt is recently returned from India."

"Ah, that explains a great deal."

Aunt Polly came in, dressed in her grubby gardening clothes. Lord Kilmore's eyebrows rose.

"Aunt Polly, this is Lord Kilmore. I am not Miss Larkin here, sir, but Miss Alison. My aunt is Miss Larkin."

He bowed to Aunt Polly's nervous curtsy. "India?" he enquired, his voice incredulous.

"No, Aunt Zenobia was in India. She is not here. I have four aunts."

"I see." Ignoring Aunt Polly, his lordship begged for the pleasure of Miss Alison's company for a drive in his curricle.

Alison eyed him consideringly. She did not care for his attitude. What was more, driving with him from Lady Emma's house along the fashionable streets to the busy Park was a very different matter from setting out through the slums to an unnamed destination. She remembered his not quite spotless reputation. "Thank you, my lord, but I had best not. I am needed here at present."

Once more he bowed. "Then allow me to express my fervent desire for your swift return to civilization. Your servant, Miss Alison." Without a word to her aunt, he departed.

"What a very fine gentleman," Aunt Polly ventured.

"Fine? He was abominably rude. But he is excessively amusing if you do not take him seriously. I daresay he will not come here again." The thought did not disturb her.

Lady Emma was a much more welcome visitor. She brought news from the world Alison had almost begun to think of as her own. Lady Castlereagh regretted Miss Larkin's absence from Almack's, she reported, but thoroughly approved of her solicitude for her elderly relative. Numerous people had enquired after her and hoped that she would not be away too long. Fanny sent countless messages and even Robert had asked his sister to convey his compliments.

Mr. Osborne also appeared in Great Ormond Street, "to check up on me," groaned Alison. The second time he came, he and Lady Emma arrived at the same moment. Alison thought they both looked rather self-conscious. They seemed to have little to say to each other, but when they departed Lady Emma offered to take Mr. Osborne up in her landau.

Alison remembered Aunt Zenobia's last letter. Mrs. Winkle, who was enjoying meeting old friends in Cheltenham, was ready to return at a moment's notice as soon as she heard that her niece was betrothed to Ralph Osborne. Whose champion was Lady Emma? Alison wondered. Was she really trying to help her protégée to marry a lord, or did she favour the odious Mr. Osborne? Was it possible she had slandered Lord Kilmore to promote the nabob's chances?

There was one regular visitor who aroused no uncomfortable reflections. Mr. Trevelyan called daily, often bearing hothouse fruit for the invalid. Alison had no qualms about accepting his invitations to drive out.

It was Mr. Trevelyan who came to fetch her when at last Aunt Cleo was recovered sufficiently for Aunt Di to return to running the household.

"You are very silent," he observed, turning onto Upper Guilford Street, past the walls of the Foundling Hospital. "You have mixed feelings, I expect, on leaving home again."

She smiled at him gratefully. "I should have known you would understand. It seems different this time, somehow. Of course I am glad that Aunt Cleo is better, and I know I shall enjoy the parties and balls, so I should be perfectly happy. But home has changed, or perhaps I have changed, and much as I love my aunts I do not quite fit there anymore."

"You have begun to see your home through the eyes of others. It is a difficult part of growing up."

"You must not think that I despise it!"

"Of course you do not."

"Lord Kilmore does. I could see quite plainly that he held my home and family in contempt. And Neil thought everything vastly funny, and Lord Fane was uneasy and condescending. You are the only gentleman who was not in some way insulting."

"You must not hold it against them. I am the only one who has had a chance to come to know your aunts. I admire them greatly, for their many good qualities but especially for what they have done for the boys. My committee has been sitting for some months now and... I shall not distress you with details of the wretched lives led by so many poor children in London. To have saved even a few from that fate is a worthwhile accomplishment."

"Can nothing be done for all the others?"

"It is a problem of proportions that only the government can tackle, and I am ashamed to say that the government sees it only in terms of crime, not of misery."

"But you are a Tory, are you not? A member of the government?"

"My family has been Tory for generations. To begin with I followed in my father's footprints without questioning, and then the Whigs' willingness to give in to Bonaparte made me sure that I was right in supporting the party that was ready to fight. Since the end of the war I have been asking the questions I should perhaps have asked earlier. In my small way I have been striving for reform from within the government. It begins to seem hopeless. I've not told anyone else, Alison, but I am seriously considering changing my allegiance."

"The Whigs are not in power. Would you not lose your post?"

"Is that so important?"

"No, it is important that you should do what you feel is right. And if you might be able to help boys like Bubble and Squeak, then I am glad." She watched his serious profile as he guided the chestnuts through the busy traffic of Oxford Street. What an admirable man he was! It was an honour to be his friend. "And I am glad you told me," she added simply.

Her contentment lasted until she had reached the house in Park Street, taken leave of Philip and stepped into the drawing-room to greet Lady Emma. She found her chaperon tête-à-tête with Mr. Ralph Osborne.

There was definitely a conspiracy afoot!

CHAPTER THIRTEEN

MR. OSBORNE STAYED ONLY long enough after Alison's arrival to ask after her aunts. As soon as he left, she turned to Lady Emma.

"I shall not marry him, even if Lord Fane does not come up to scratch."

"Pray do not use that vulgar phrase, Alison. I cannot understand why you are determined against Mr. Osborne. I assure you that though he is Mrs. Winkle's agent, he has your interests at heart. He is a kind, commonsensical gentleman, and as rich and good-looking as any girl could want."

"Yes, he would be an excellent uncle. It is a pity that my aunts are as much too old for him as he is too old for me."

That made Lady Emma laugh, but she said soberly, "You do not think that Mrs. Winkle will insist on your marrying him? She does like to have her way."

"Aunt Zenobia cannot force me to the altar, and I believe she is too generous to threaten me with poverty if I dislike the marriage. Nor can she force Mr. Osborne to offer for me. He certainly does not act as if he is in love with me, so perhaps he will not even go so far as to ask for my hand."

"I understood there was an agreement between them."

Alison thought back to the moment when Aunt Zenobia had disclosed her plans. "My aunt said that she did not mean to 'push' me, only that he would be glad to make a match with me. I doubt there is any formal agreement. She told me that I need not hunt for a husband, not that I must not. She cannot have promised Mr. Osborne my hand, and surely he cannot have promised to take me before he even met me."

"I see." Lady Emma sounded relieved.

"You must not worry that Aunt Zenobia will be angry with you if I refuse to wed him," Alison assured her. "I shall tell her that my decision is not at all your fault, so you can stop plotting with him to advance his suit."

"No more plotting," she agreed, but the twinkle in her eyes belied her gravity. "However, you must not expect me to cut the acquaintance of a sudden. It would be unpardonably rude, and besides, he has a right and a duty to see to your welfare in Mrs. Winkle's absence. And I enjoy his company."

"I do not *dislike* him, I just do not want to marry him."

"Of course not, he is not a lord. Enough of Mr. Osborne. I fear you are in for a dull evening. I was not sure when you would return here so I accepted a dinner invitation for tonight."

"Never mind, I am used to retiring early after being at home," said Alison philosophically.

After Lady Emma's departure, she ate a solitary meal before the fire in the drawing-room. She had taken up a book and Henry was clearing away the dishes when the door knocker sounded. He hurried to answer it.

Returning a moment later, he announced, "It's Lord Kilmore, miss, wants a word with you."

"Lord Kilmore! At this hour? Good gracious, I cannot receive him here alone. I had best slip into the hall and see what he wants."

His lordship looked particularly dashing, with a black domino draped over his evening clothes and a black mask dangling from his hand. A second domino, of pale blue silk, was folded over his other arm.

"Miss Alison," he greeted her, bowing. She was not sure that she approved of his continued use of her Christian name. "I happened to hear that you were returned to the world today. It is the luckiest chance. There is a masquerade tonight at Vauxhall."

"Thank you, my lord, for remembering that I wanted to attend a masquerade, but I cannot go. Lady Emma is gone out." Alison could not help sounding disappointed.

"Ah, but I have thought of everything. Not only have I brought a domino for you, I have a chaperon waiting in the carriage outside."

"A chaperon?"

"You are acquainted with Mrs. Darnell, I believe? She and her husband will go with us."

"I have only met Mr. Darnell." Alison remembered him as a respectable, somewhat stout gentleman of middle years, who seemed an unlikely companion for Lord Kilmore. However, his wife must be an acceptable chaperon, she thought. She *did* want to go to a masquerade. "Thank you, sir, I will go. Pray ask the Darnells to step in while I change my dress."

"That is not necessary. You look enchanting as you are, and the domino will hide everything anyway." He held the light, hooded cloak out to her.

"No, it would be shocking to go out for the evening in a morning gown," she said, laughing. "I shall not keep you above a quarter hour, I promise."

He looked annoyed, but acquiesced and sent Harry out to fetch his friends while Alison ran upstairs with the domino. She called Carter to help her change.

"I'm sure I don't know what her ladyship'll think," said the abigail worriedly, undoing the row of tiny buttons down the back of Alison's gown. "Going off with a gentleman at this time of night. The blue sarcenet you want to wear?"

"Yes, to match the domino. There will be a perfectly unexceptionable couple with us, or I should not go. I shall write a note to Lady Emma, so pray do not be anxious, Carter dear. No, I do not need a hat, as the domino has a hood. There, that is perfect, thank you." She sat down at her little writing table and dashed off a brief explanation. Sanding and folding the sheet, she handed it to the abigail. "Give that to Lady Emma as soon as she comes in, if you please."

When Alison reached the drawing-room, she was dismayed to find that though Mr. Darnell was as she recalled him, his wife was something of a surprise. Wrapped in a scarlet domino that matched her lips, she was a brassy blonde with improbably dark eyebrows and lashes.

Lord Kilmore presented Alison to her.

"Nice to meet you, dearie," she said. "His lordship said you was pretty as a picture and I can see he told no lie. Let's be off, then, or we'll miss the Cascade. Did you ever see the Cascade, dearie?"

In the face of such friendliness, Alison did not know how to say that she had changed her mind.

As if aware of her uneasiness, Lord Kilmore was at his most charming and solicitous. He did not attempt to flirt, helping her into the carriage with no more than a steadying hand beneath her elbow. As they drove towards the river, he apologized that short notice had prevented hiring a boat to complete the enjoyment of the evening. Instead they crossed the Thames by the new Vauxhall Bridge, joining a stream of carriages heading in the same direction.

When the coachman drew up at the entrance to the gardens, Lord Kilmore pulled a mask from his pocket and begged Alison's permission to help her tie it on. She pushed back the hood of the domino and held the strip of blue satin to her face while he tied the ribbons among her curls. His fingers were deft, scarcely touching her head, and she began to relax.

"Can you see, Miss Larkin?" he enquired.

She adjusted the mask. It felt odd, but she could see perfectly well. Following the Darnells, he helped her down from the carriage. She took his arm, he paid the entrance fee, and they walked with the crowds into the gardens.

"Oh, it is delightful!" breathed Alison, gazing around at the coloured lamps hanging from the trees, the colonnades and pavilions, all thronged with multihued dominoes. The strains of music drifted on the breeze from a nearby building. "Can we go and hear the orchestra?"

"Of course, my dear, if you are not hungry. I did succeed in reserving a box for supper."

"I have eaten, but perhaps you have not, ma'am?" She turned to Mrs. Darnell.

"Not to worry, dearie. You go and listen to the music with his lordship. Me and Darnell'll find the box and you can come along when you're good and ready. Don't be late for the Cascade, mind, and then there's the fireworks at midnight. You won't want to miss them." She tugged on her husband's arm, and before Alison could protest they had vanished in the crowd.

"I fear Mrs. Darnell has not the refinement one might wish," said Lord Kilmore ruefully. "She is kind-hearted, however. By all means let us go to the Music Room. The building itself is worth a visit."

The circular room, with its flowery, canopy-styled ceiling, was very fine. Alison had never seen a musical ensemble larger than a dance band before and she enjoyed watching the players as much as listening to Handel's tuneful "Water Music." Lord Kilmore told her the history of the piece.

"Handel was court composer to the Elector of Hanover," he explained. "He came to visit England and was so lionized he decided to stay. Then the poor fellow found that the patron he had deserted was about to become King George I of England. Can you picture his despair? Doubtless he would have torn his hair had he possessed any, but of course they wore wigs in those days."

Alison giggled. "Did he win back the king's favour?" she asked.

"He wrote the music you have just heard and had it played on a boat on the Thames, following the royal barge. George expressed his delight too forcefully to be able to renege when he discovered that the composer was his faithless servant."

"I'm glad, and not a bit surprised. The music was splendid and it must have sounded even better heard across the water." Alison was quite in charity with

Lord Kilmore as they strolled back towards the supper boxes.

Nonetheless, she was relieved to find the Darnells waiting there for them, though the gentleman's eyes were somewhat glazed and his nose bid fair to rival the red of his wife's domino.

"There you are, dearie," Mrs. Darnell greeted her. "Nice music, was it? I'm fond of a good tune myself. You've just time for a bite of supper before the Cascade."

Alison was not hungry, but she could not refuse to taste Vauxhall's famous wafer-thin ham. She did refuse to sip of the equally famous arrack punch, in which Mr. Darnell had been overindulging during their absence, and she turned down champagne in favour of lemonade. Lord Kilmore did not press her. Her last suspicions vanished.

Mr. Darnell was quietly snoozing in a corner of the booth by the time people began to stream towards the Cascade. His wife was perfectly willing to abandon him rather than miss her favourite spectacle. Alison was glad of her presence on one side and Lord Kilmore's on the other, for the mannerly, elegant crowd was changing character.

Many women had abandoned their dominoes to expose barely decent dresses, and they hung on the arms of their cavaliers, giggling and shrieking. Lord Kilmore steered her away from the most blatant excesses.

"Alas, Vauxhall is not the exclusive place it once was," he said. "I hope you feel its attractions outweigh its disadvantages, Miss Larkin."

"It is prodigious amusing," she assured him, trying not to notice that Mrs. Darnell's domino had fallen

open to reveal a décolleté so deep it was a wonder her
gown did not fall off.

"You mustn't mind them, dearie. Just having a bit
of fun, like. Wait till you see the Cascade."

The much-vaunted Cascade proved worthy of its
fame. Alison gazed entranced, exclaiming in delight as
a country scene in miniature passed before their eyes,
propelled by a water-wheel. She was aware that his
lordship was watching her, not the spectacle, amused
by her raptures.

"I have never seen anything like it," she explained,
glancing up at him.

He smiled, his eyes warm. "I am gratified to have
pleased you."

The show over, they returned towards the supper
box. They had nearly reached it when Mrs. Darnell,
with a cry of "Georgie, my dove," swooped on a
passing gentleman.

"Why, Ginger, sweetheart, where the devil have you
been?" he responded, bussing her cheek and putting
his arm about her waist. Far from objecting, she
glanced back and winked at Alison and Lord Kilmore,
then swayed closer.

"I had to find a chaperon in a hurry. My choice was
not ideal," Lord Kilmore admitted. "She is lively
company, though, and I fear it will be dull with only
her husband. The fireworks do not begin until midnight. There are some very pretty grottoes and temples
scattered about the grounds; do you care to go exploring?"

PHILIP TREVELYAN HAD BEEN surprised to meet Lady
Emma at the Lansdownes'. Her family was as Tory as
his own. While dinner with the Marquis of Lans-

downe was not an outright declaration of Whig sympathies, as a visit to Holland House would be, tonight's gathering was of a political nature.

Emma's companion surprised Philip less. Osborne had mentioned his interest in offering financial support to the party of parliamentary reform, and Philip had, in fact, supplied the merchant's introduction to the marquis. That Ralph Osborne had escorted Emma was not so much surprising as intriguing. Especially as Emma did not quite meet Philip's eyes when she expressed her pleasure at seeing him there.

He had no leisure to observe the pair, for his own presence was an exploratory foray. It took all his skill to discover, without making any definite commitment, what his reception might be if he switched parties.

He was satisfied with the results. Alison would be glad to hear that he was making progress with the plans for his political future. As it was not late when the company dispersed, he decided to go with Lady Emma and her escort back to Park Street in the hope of finding Alison still downstairs so that he could tell her. Not until they reached the house did he realize how odd it would look to be asking to see a young lady at eleven o'clock in the evening.

"May I offer you a glass of brandy, gentlemen?" Lady Emma suggested. "The night is still young."

It would not be proper for either of them to accept alone. Philip exchanged a glance with Osborne and was pleased when the other nodded.

"That sounds like a splendid notion, Emma," he said with alacrity.

They had scarcely descended from the landau when the front door swung open. The footman ran down the steps to meet them.

"My lady! Mrs. Carter has a letter for you. It's Miss Alison, she went off wi' the gentleman."

Emma's abigail was standing in the doorway waving a paper. Philip took the steps in two strides and whipped it from her hand. He was about to unfold the note when it dawned on him that he had not the slightest right to do anything of the sort. On tenterhooks, he passed it on to Emma.

She moved into the hall, Osborne close behind.

"What does it say?" demanded Philip impatiently.

"Miss Alison went off with Lord Kilmore," the abigail announced.

"Hush, Carter." Emma was a little pale. "Yes, she has gone with Kilmore, to a masquerade. At Vauxhall," she added faintly. Osborne helped her to a chair.

"Alone with that libertine?" Philip raged. "The little shatterbrain!"

"Not alone. She says that a respectable couple is to go with them. Oh lord, the Darnells!"

"The Darnells?" Osborne enquired. "Who are they?"

"He will be under the table within the hour," Emma explained.

"And she will be under the bushes with the first coxcomb who blows her a kiss," Philip added. "Begging your pardon, Emma. I'll take your carriage, and pray God I do not arrive too late."

"I'm coming with you," said Osborne grimly. "Alison is my responsibility. Try not to worry, Lady Emma. We shall bring her home safe and sound, I make no doubt."

Half-way back to the carriage already, Philip snorted as he heard those words of comfort behind him. Kilmore was in Dun Territory, and if he could compromise Alison so that she had to marry him, he would not think twice about it. Fear twisted Philip's innards as he jumped up onto the box and dispossessed the coachman of the reins. Osborne just managed to scramble aboard before the landau rocked into motion.

An elegant but clumsy landau pulled by two showy but sluggish steeds was not precisely the vehicle Philip would have chosen for a dash to the rescue. However, it carried them in one piece to Vauxhall Gardens. Osborne emerged from the interior looking somewhat shaken, and glanced around.

"I've never been here," he said as they passed through the entrance, unwatched at this late hour. "Where do we begin the search?"

Philip shrugged, angry to feel so helpless. "It's only in the dark walks that she is likely to be in serious trouble, but that is the most difficult place to find anyone. We shall have to separate and do the best we can. You go round to the left." He pulled out his watch and opened it. "The fireworks will begin in about twenty minutes. We'd best meet there to search the crowds."

They were about to split up when Philip felt a tug on his sleeve.

"Guv!"

He looked down into the anxious freckled face of Tarry Joe. "What the devil?"

"I bin lookin' fer ya, guv. I knowed one o' you gentry coves'd come after 'er."

CHAPTER FOURTEEN

"I DO THINK WE OUGHT TO rearrange him," said Alison. "He looks shockingly uncomfortable and he will soon be on the floor."

Lord Kilmore obligingly lifted Mr. Darnell's feet and laid him out flat on the bench. "How fortunate that we are not a large party," he observed.

"Yes, only think if we had two or three gentlemen in the same condition. There would be nowhere to put them. This syllabub is quite delicious," she added, returning to the dish before her. "Do you suppose they would give me the receipt for Aunt Cleo?"

"There's no harm in trying." With some invisible signal he summoned a waiter.

He was consulting the man when Alison caught sight of Philip Trevelyan coming towards their booth, followed by Ralph Osborne. Happy to see at least the former, she waved. The barely suppressed anger on Philip's face turned to sardonic amusement, while Mr. Osborne's anxiety gave way to wrath.

Alison touched Lord Kilmore's arm. "Look, my lord, Mr. Trevelyan is here."

Dismissing the waiter, he sighed. "Just when we were congratulating ourselves on being a small party. What do you suggest, ma'am, shall we prop Darnell in a corner or put him under the table? Servant, Trevelyan. Evening, Osborne."

The two gentlemen nodded stiffly as Alison giggled. "Leave the poor man be. It is almost time for the fireworks." She smiled up at Philip. "I am happy to see you, sir. Is not this a delightful place?"

"Delightful!" Mr. Osborne exploded. "Are you aware, young woman—"

"Delightful indeed," Philip interrupted him. "However, Lady Emma is in some concern as to your well-being. Doubtless his lordship will excuse you."

"But the fireworks will begin at any moment. I do so want to see them."

His lordship lounged back, looking satirical, toying with his wineglass and taking no part in the argument.

"Fireworks?" said Mr. Osborne. "By Jove, I have always wanted to see a firework display."

"You may stay. I shall take Miss Alison home."

"Please let me stay, too. I may never have another chance and Lady Emma will know that I am safe, since you are here."

"Another half hour will make no difference, Trevelyan." Mr. Osborne agreed with Alison. "You must be aware that I would not do anything to distress Lady Emma."

At that moment the waiter returned, handed Lord Kilmore a slip of paper and received a shilling for his pains. His lordship turned to Alison.

"The syllabub receipt, Miss Larkin. Are these rude fellows troubling you? Shall I sent them to the right-about?"

"Oh no, pray do not." Though she was not sure what he intended, it did not sound like a good idea. She tucked the paper in her reticule. "But I *should* like to see the fireworks," she repeated hopefully.

"And I should not dream of depriving you of that pleasure. Come, it is time to take our places if we wish for a good view." Standing up, he stepped out of the box, forcing Philip and Mr. Osborne to move back. He offered his arm to Alison and she laid her hand on it.

Short of starting a mêlée, there was nothing the others could do but follow as they made their way to the viewing stands.

Alison was glad that she had insisted. The incandescent splendour of Roman candles, Catherine wheels, rockets bursting in the air in showers of red and green and gold sparkles, the pops and bangs and fizzes—all was magical. She clung to Lord Kilmore's arm, but she was comfortingly aware of Philip and Mr. Osborne behind her, sheltering her from the rowdy crowd. The set piece at the end, recognizable busts of the Duke of Wellington and the Prince of Wales, called forth mingled boos and cheers. A fist-fight started not far off.

"Time to go," said Lord Kilmore.

With a determined triple escort, it was not difficult to escape the throng. No sooner had they a little space about them than Philip turned to his lordship.

"I shall take Miss Larkin home."

"If you insist. I daresay I ought to make some attempt to find my other guests."

Alison held out her hand to Lord Kilmore. "I have enjoyed myself excessively, sir. It was prodigious kind in you to invite me."

"My pleasure, Miss Alison." He raised her hand to his lips and kissed it, his breath warming her fingers through her glove, his enigmatic gaze holding hers.

All the way back to Park Street, Mr. Osborne lectured Alison on her duty to Lady Emma. She bore the scold in near silence, venturing an occasional subdued protest. Philip said nothing. When they reached the house, he helped her down.

Mr. Osborne followed. "I shall have to find a hackney," he said irritably. "Tell her ladyship I shall call tomorrow."

"I shall tell her." As she spoke, Alison saw a slight figure jump down from the back of the carriage. A freckled face appeared momentarily and a gold coin spun towards it, glittering in the gas light.

Mr. Osborne strode off into the night. Alison turned to Philip.

"That was Tarry Joe!"

"He, too, is concerned for your safety."

"You need not have worried about me. Lord Kilmore was all that is gentlemanly and you were disgracefully rude to him. Besides, '*Timeo Danaos, et dona ferentes.*' But I was having a splendid time!"

"'*Timeo...*'?" he began, but the front door opened and she flounced up the steps and into the house.

Lady Emma was hurrying out of the drawing-room as she entered the hall.

"My dear, are you all right?"

"Oh yes, perfectly." She ran to hug her chaperon. "I did not mean to distress you. When I realized how unsuitable the Darnells were it was too late. I could not say, 'I am sorry, but after seeing you I cannot go,' and I did not know what to do. However, Lord Kilmore was altogether chivalrous and Vauxhall was beyond anything great."

"But a masquerade!"

"I did not know it was improper to go to a masquerade at Vauxhall. I do not remember that you ever told me."

"Probably not, because no one ever invited you. Still, I daresay no one was there who might have recognized you."

"I was wearing a mask all evening—I took it off in the carriage—and I kept the hood of my domino up. Lord Kilmore brought it for me. Is it not pretty?"

"Just your colour." Lady Emma combined a smile with a sigh and a shake of the head. "All's well that ends well, I suppose. At least you had the sense to leave word for me."

"To tell the truth," Alison confided, "I was not at all sorry to see Mr. Trevelyan."

ALISON WAS NEITHER SORRY nor surprised, when she rose late the next morning, that though Lady Emma was still abed, Philip was awaiting her in the breakfast parlour. Henry's shrug told her he was no match for Mr. Trevelyan. He brought her usual eggs and toast, poured a cup of tea and stood fiddling aimlessly at the sideboard.

"You may go, Henry. I've no intention of assaulting Miss Alison over the breakfast table."

The footman flushed and glanced at Alison.

"Thank you, Henry, I shall not need you for a while." The moment the door closed behind him she turned to Philip and said in a militant voice, "There is no need to bully the servants only because you wish to haul me over the coals. I suppose that *is* why you have invited yourself to breakfast?"

"No. As a matter of fact I want to ask you what you meant by '*Timeo Danaos*' et cetera."

Astonished, she asked, "Did you not learn Latin in school?"

"Don't be pert—I beg your pardon, I should not have said that. Yes, I did learn Latin, but you did not go to school, and if you had you would have studied sketching, not Latin. I just wanted to know what you meant by that tag."

" 'I fear the Greeks, even bearing gifts.' Laocoön said that when the Trojans decided to pull the wooden horse into the city. Lord Kilmore offered me something I wanted, but that does not mean I trusted him. I was on my guard."

"Look what happened to Laocoön."

"Strangled by a sea serpent. That was most unfair of the gods, particularly as it squished his sons, too."

"For heaven's sake, Alison, forget Laocoön, forget Kilmore, where did you learn Latin? I have been puzzling over it all night."

"I told you that my grandfather was a classical scholar. He left hundreds of books—that is why we never use the back parlour for guests. Many of them were in Greek and I never quite worked out the alphabet. There were Latin dictionaries and translations, though, and I managed to pick up enough to read quite a number of the books. One cannot be forever reading romances, you know."

"I never guessed you were a bluestocking."

"One cannot be forever spouting Latin quotations, either, and Lady Emma warned me particularly to avoid doing so. Do you mind that I am a bluestocking?" she asked wistfully. "I am not, really, for I am woefully ignorant about most things."

"Mind? Why should I mind? You are the most extraordinary woman I have ever met."

The intensity of his gaze made her lower her eyes. It was a relief when the door opened and Lady Emma came in wearing an elegant wrapper and looking flustered.

"Alison, it is not at all proper—"

"My fault, Emma. I suppose the watch-servant reported to you."

"If you mean that my footman has more concern for the proprieties than you do, then you are right." She sat down at the table. "Really, Philip, I do not know what has come over you. You used to be the soul of decorum. That you have a bone to pick with Alison after last night is no excuse."

He looked amused. "The bone is picked. My apologies, and I am on my way. I shall see you this evening?"

"At the Hardcastles' ball? Yes."

"Then each of you reserve a waltz for me, if you please. Good day, ladies." He swept them a half-mocking bow and was gone.

"I declare I scarcely recognize Philip. He seems to grow younger instead of older. I hope he did not ring a peal over you?"

"Not exactly," said Alison.

She had no leisure to ponder Mr. Trevelyan's odd behaviour, for Lord Fane came to call.

Alison was *aux anges*. He had not deserted her after all. In fact, he even asked after the health of her aunt and, as they drove through the Park, told her something of the business that had taken him into the country.

"One has a duty to one's tenants and a duty to the land," he explained. "Fane Hall has been in the family for over three centuries. It is a weighty responsibility."

"I am certain your tenants have nothing to complain of in their landlord," she assured him.

"I think not. However, I do not mean to oppress you with ideas a pretty young female cannot be expected to comprehend. Do you go the Hardcastles' tonight? I trust I have not returned to Town so late as to find you engaged already for the entire evening?"

With a becoming show of modesty, Alison agreed to save him two dances. Before they left the Park another two gentlemen, delighted to see her back in circulation, had asked her to stand up with them. Displaying every sign of jealousy, Lord Fane refused to stop to allow a third to approach them. It was all very flattering, and she could hardly wait to tell Lady Emma.

Her usually cautious chaperon had to agree that Lord Fane's attentions were becoming most particular. "I begin to believe you will see a lord at your feet after all," she said, laughing. "I hope you will invite me to the wedding, and that we shall be friends when you are married."

It was then that Alison realized she had never thought beyond the delightful moment when a romantic lord would vow eternal devotion.

Did she really want to spend the rest of her life with Lord Fane? With Lord Kilmore? Even with dear Neil, if he had not had his Bridey waiting for him? Was it really so romantic to marry a lord?

She liked Philip better than any of them.

And then there were the unexplained and unmentionable aspects of a wife's duties. She had been vaguely aware, that evening at Vauxhall, that the disgraceful goings-on had something to do with that mysterious business. Mrs. Darnell and the other im-

modest females she had seen had been enjoying themselves, so presumably the experience was pleasant, but
she could not imagine herself making so free with Lord
Fane, even as his wife. With Philip, on the other hand,
exploring the subject might prove interesting. With
Philip, life in general would be—interesting.

He had said she was extraordinary. Suddenly it was
very important to know what he meant by that word.

"My dear, you have fallen into a brown study."
Lady Emma interrupted her musing. "I said, let us go
up and make sure nothing needs to be done to your ball
gown before this evening."

"Yes, it must be perfect tonight," Alison eagerly
agreed. Tonight, waltzing with Philip, she would ask
him what he meant.

CHAPTER FIFTEEN

THE BALL GOWN was perfect. Carter had sewed fresh lace edging on the white sarcenet and replaced trailing green ribbons with dozens of minute blue bows, arranged to form rosettes. Nonetheless, Alison went to the wardrobe and took out her first ball gown, the white with silver net. The first time she wore it Philip had called her an enchanting elf.

"There's a tear in the sleeve of that one, miss," Carter reported. "I've not had time to mend it, being as I was refurbishing this. And her ladyship said as you might want to change the net for a bit of blue gauze."

"I do not want ever to change it." Regretfully she hung the gown up. "This one is very pretty too. Thank you for all your work."

"I've saved a bit of ribbon for your hair, miss. That blue do bring out the colour of your eyes."

Judging by the number of gentlemen at the Hardcastles' ball who commented on the brilliance of Alison's eyes, Carter was right. Lord Fane remarked significantly that they reminded him of the ornamental lake at Fane Hall on a sunny day. Lord Kilmore told her, in a soft voice, that they put to shame Lady Jersey's magnificent sapphires. Even Neil had something to say on the subject.

"Sure and if it weren't that me own eyes are the spit and image of yours...but I would not care to be caught boasting. Put me down for the first waltz, cousin. We'll dance back to back and dazzle them all.''

Laughing, Alison turned to her chaperon.

''That will do very well,'' said Lady Emma. ''Philip is not here yet, so I will write him down on my card for the first waltz and you may take the second with him.''

Alison could think of no valid reason to object. She would just have to wait to talk to him.

She stood up for the country dance just before the first waltz with the youthful Lord Mortimer Hardcastle, who had come up to Town from Cambridge to grace his parents' ball. Tall, clumsy and bashful, he gazed at her with such wistful admiration that he forgot to mind his steps. She managed to steer him safely through the set until they reached the last figure. They were turning arm in arm when there was a horrid ripping noise and a couple of feet of lace trim parted company with the hem of Alison's dress.

Lord Mortimer stopped in his tracks, appalled. Alison tugged him out of the way of the other dancers towards the side of the room, doing a sort of shuffle to avoid entangling her feet in the dangling loop of lace.

His face was scarlet, his mind obviously racing in a desperate search for words of apology which eluded him. She patted his arm.

''Never mind,'' she consoled him. ''I can pin it up. But I must go to the ladies' withdrawing-room and it will take a few minutes. Will you find my cousin, Lord Deverill, for me, and explain that I may miss our waltz?''

Lord Mortimer nodded. ''Miss Larkin, I...'' He ran out of words again.

''That's quite all right. Pray do not worry about it. I enjoyed our dance, my lord.'' She smiled at him encouragingly and went off to find the withdrawing-room.

When she returned to the ballroom, the waltz was in full swing. Neil was nowhere to be seen; she guessed he had repaired to the card room. Since Lady Emma was dancing with Philip, Alison made her way to Lady Edgehill's side.

"May I take refuge with you, ma'am? A slight accident to my skirt, and I have lost my partner."

"Of course, my dear," the countess welcomed her. "Emma is standing up with Philip, I see. A fine couple they make, do they not? One of these days Emma will come to her senses and make him happy."

"Make him happy, my lady?"

"Marry him. He has been pursuing her these three or four years, since she has been out of mourning. A most suitable match, is it not?"

"Most suitable, ma'am," said Alison faintly. How blind she had been! Feeling rather peculiar, she sat still and let Lady Edgehill's chatter wash over her.

The countess was in a communicative mood. "He has no title, to be sure, but a very old family for all that, and she had enough of aristocratic romance with Grant. I always said Stephen Grant was a handsome ne'er-do-well but she would have him. Edgehill and I were not in the least surprised when he killed himself racing a stage-coach and left her near penniless. We have known Philip Trevelyan forever and he is a steady young man, well thought of in government circles and wealthy enough to support Emma in the luxury the dear girl deserves. He would do anything for her, I believe."

Including being kind to her protégée, Alison thought. Including going out of his way to make an odd little Cit feel at home in Society. She had been warned: Lady Emma had said that Philip was always ready to put himself out for an old friend. Emma was more to him than that, though. He loved her and did not want her to suffer for her audacious attempt to foist an ill-bred, ignorant chit on the ton.

Alison squared her shoulders. It was lucky she had found out in time. And whatever Mr. Trevelyan's motive, he *had* helped to make her comfortable in this glittering world. She was not going to throw away all that she had gained.

When Neil arrived to commiserate on the missed waltz, she was all sparkling gaiety.

She danced next with Lord Kilmore, and then with Lord Fane. The nonsensical flattery of the one and the steadfast admiration of the other did much to restore her composure. By the time Philip claimed her for the waltz she was ready to hold her own in conversation, though with a sense of unreality that he did not seem to observe.

She did not ask him why he had called her extraordinary.

In the carriage going home from the Hardcastles' she took advantage of the darkness to ask Lady Emma about what her mother had said.

"I did not know that Mr. Trevelyan wanted to marry you."

"It is not something either of us is likely to bruit abroad, and it was wrong in Mama to tell you. However, since she did—yes, Philip has proposed several times."

"Do you not want to take a second husband?" Aware that her question was impertinent, Alison would not have been surprised to receive a set-down.

Lady Emma was silent for a few moments. Then she spoke, slowly, as if forced to examine her thoughts before she was able to express them. "Yes, I want to remarry. The social round becomes wearisome. It is no reflection on you, Alison. Indeed you have been quite the pleasantest of my girls. I daresay you can understand that to go to parties because one ought to, not because one chooses to, might grow tedious? Stephen—Lord Grant—was a very sociable person. He was handsome and dashing and romantic, all the qualities that sweep a young girl off her feet, but he was not dependable. He was not even kind, except in a careless way. I want a husband who is considerate of my feelings, and above all one who is practical. Someone who solves problems instead of creating them."

Philip was kind and dependable. Philip considered the feelings even of eccentric maiden aunts, while he solved their problems with aplomb. He was undoubtedly just what Lady Emma wanted.

Alison sighed.

IT WAS CHEERING the next morning to find not one but three bouquets of red roses awaiting her in the breakfast parlour. Their fragrance overwhelmed the odours of toast and ham.

"Who are they from?" asked Lady Emma.

Alison read the cards. "The buds are from Lord Fane. I do not know the language of flowers but I should guess that buds indicate caution?"

"Uncertainty, perhaps."

"The biggest bouquet is from Lord Mortimer Hardcastle. His pen is readier than his tongue. He apologizes for stepping on my hem and then he writes,

'I shall be finished at the university in just one more year.' What do you suppose that signifies?''

"The poor boy is smitten but does not quite dare ask you to wait for him.''

"After one dance, during which he scarce opened his mouth! Oh dear.''

"Calf-love. He will be over it long before he takes his degree. And the third?''

"From Lord Kilmore.'' Alison felt her cheeks grow warm. "He begs for an opportunity to speak to me privately.''

"So the moment has come,'' said Lady Emma, looking thoughtful. "To tell the truth, I do not know what to advise you. A month ago—a week ago—I should have warned you to beware. Now I am not so sure.''

"What has changed your opinion, ma'am?''

She shrugged. "He ought not to have taken you to Vauxhall, but his behaviour there was unexceptionable. Because of that, I observed him closely last night. I am prepared to believe that he has a genuine affection for you, not only for your fortune. You might do worse. You like him, do you not?''

"He is charming and amusing,'' said Alison cautiously.

"Who knows, you might be happy with him. I cannot presume to say. I must tell you that I discussed the matter with Ral...Mr. Osborne last night.''

"I did not see him at the ball.''

"He came only for a short time. He is certain that he can tie up your money so as to keep the bulk of it from your husband's hands. Under those circumstances, Kilmore might be an acceptable match.''

"Or he might cry off.''

Lady Emma smiled. "That is always possible. You need not see him alone if you do not wish it. I shall tell him that his suit is not welcome. But I must point out that whatever your decision, this may be your only opportunity to see a lord at your feet. We cannot count on Fane."

"It would hardly be fair to Lord Kilmore to agree to listen to him only for that reason! Still, if he really is fond of me perhaps I should marry him. At least I owe him the courtesy of a personal answer. Not today though—I promised to go shopping with Fanny, and Lord Fane is to drive me in the Park later."

Alison still had not made up her mind what the answer should be when at last, four days later, Lord Kilmore obtained his interview with her.

Henry had his instructions. Not five minutes after his lordship was shown into the drawing-room, scarce time to exchange greetings and remarks about the weather (prodigious fine for early May), the footman informed Lady Emma that the housekeeper had urgent need of her.

"Pray excuse me for a few minutes," she said and made a graceful exit.

Alison could not help feeling that the whole affair smacked a little too much of stage management. Not one of Mrs. Meeke's heroines had ever plotted beforehand with her chaperon to ensure a private moment with the hero. In fact, she could not recall that any of Mrs. Meeke's heroines, or Mrs. Cuthbertson's for that matter, had a chaperon. However, she set aside her sewing and awaited the sequel with interest.

Lord Kilmore had politely stood with Lady Emma. He now took a turn about the room, glanced out of the window, fiddled with one of the ornaments on the mantel and tugged at his cravat. He could not be said to exude wild-eyed passion, but Alison found his uncertainty touching. A fortune hunter surely ought to be smooth and self-possessed.

"Miss Larkin!" He swung round, making her start. "Miss Alison!"

"My lord!" The words that should have rung with a thrilling tone emerged sounding prim.

In two strides he was before her, sinking to one knee and seizing her hand in his. This was more promising. The light in his dark eyes was warm, if not quite burning.

"Alison, marry me! I cannot live without you. You are quite the sweetest, prettiest, most enchanting creature I have ever met."

Richest, added a voice in her head. Her response was involuntary. "Do you not mean that you cannot live without my fortune?" she asked sadly.

"My wretched reputation goes before me." His expression was rueful. Rising from his knee, he took a seat beside her on the sofa, still holding her hand. "I confess that at first I pursued you more for my creditors' sake than my own. I was only too pleased to find an heiress who was not muffin-faced and whose background, I hoped, might frighten off more eligible suitors than I. Don't be offended, I am attempting to be honest."

"That first evening, at my ball, when you did not speak to me, you were trying to pique my interest?"

He grinned wryly. "I succeeded, did I not? I thought to catch you in a net, but instead, as I came to know you, I was caught myself in a silken web. I meant what I said, Alison. You are enchanting, I have never known a woman like you, and I want you to be my wife."

His dark hair was ruffled where he had run his fingers through it, his eyes serious, without their usual teasing light. His hand, holding hers, was lean and strong and warm. He looked very romantic.

Alison was tempted.

CHAPTER SIXTEEN

"SO YOU REJECTED HIM after all," said Lady Emma.

"Yes." Alison sighed. "I do believe he has a decided partiality for me, and he is excessively attractive, but I simply do not want to be married to him."

"I trust he did not take umbrage at your refusal?"

"No, he did not seem to be miffed. Regretful, rather. He said he hopes we may remain friends. I told him I like him very well, just that I do not think we should suit."

"He seems to have behaved very handsomely, better than one might have expected considering his circumstances."

"I wish I could have offered him money to pay his debts, but it would not have been proper, would it?"

"Certainly not! I daresay Kilmore will come about. Nor would Ralph—Mr. Osborne have countenanced such a thing short of marriage. I begin to think that whomever you wed he had best tie up your fortune, or you will be giving it away to the first beggar on your doorstep."

"Neil would not accept anything from me."

"My opinion of your cousin rises by leaps and bounds." Lady Emma looked round as the footman came in. "What is it, Henry? We are at home to visitors now."

"It's one o' them brats, my lady, brought a note for Miss Alison." He handed a twist of paper to Alison and whispered out of the side of his mouth, "Bubble, miss. I sent him to the kitchen for a bite." He winked, enjoying the conspiracy. His mistress did not appreciate the boys' presence in her house.

"Thank you, Henry." Alison unfolded the note. "It's from Aunt Cleo. Oh dear, Aunt Di has sprained her ankle. Nothing serious, but Aunt Cleo says she ought not to be walking Midnight, and he must go out." She turned to Lady Emma. "He will not go with anyone else but me."

"Send round for the carriage, Henry," said Lady Emma resignedly. "I do not need to go anywhere today, fortunately. I hope you will not be too long, though, Alison. Are you not expecting Lord Fane this afternoon?"

"Yes, and Neil and Fanny too, which means of course that Robert will come." She glanced at the ormolu clock on the mantel. The interview with Lord Kilmore had taken longer than she thought. "Pray make my excuses if I am a little late."

It was a beautiful day, sunny and warm with a light breeze, and walking was a pleasure even in the brick fields. Alison wondered what it would be like to live in the country. Midnight would be able to roam free, to run after rabbits and swim in the streams. He was bred to enjoy water, and she often regretted that she could not let him dive into the New River Head reservoir on the far side of the fields.

Lord Fane had an ornamental lake at his country home. Would he allow Midnight to swim in it? Would he even want Midnight at Fane Hall?

She had seen dogs swimming in the Serpentine in Hyde Park. Perhaps tomorrow she might bundle Midnight into the landau and take him there. Now *that* would shock Lord Fane if he saw her! Philip—Mr. Trevelyan, on the other hand, had taken the dog up in his own tilbury and had walked with her across these very fields. But she had vowed to put Mr. Trevelyan out of her mind.

That was not easy, when she saw him as often as ever. In fact, when she returned to Park Street he was among the company awaiting her.

"Miss Witherington's come," Henry advised her as she stepped into the house, "and Mr. Gilchrist, of course. Lord Fane, Lord Deverill, Mr. Trevelyan, Mr. Osborne. An excess o' gentlemen, that's what I likes to see."

"I beg your pardon for my tardiness," Alison said gaily as she entered the crowded drawing-room. "I expect Lady Emma explained that I had to go home to walk my aunt's dog."

Judging by Lord Fane's face, that was not precisely the excuse Lady Emma had given, and he was far from certain that he approved.

"You will be too tired to walk in the Park then," said Fanny, disappointed. "Mr. Gilchrist and I were hoping to persuade you to go with us. It is such a lovely day."

"Tired? Heavens no. But I must not desert our other guests." She looked enquiringly at Lord Fane.

"I shall be happy to lend you my arm, Miss Larkin, if you are sure you are not fatigued."

Lady Emma gave her permission but said she was expecting Mrs. Talmadge and would not go. Mr. Trevelyan and Mr. Osborne elected to stay, but Neil chose to go with them—"to play gooseberry," he said wickedly as soon as the front door closed behind them.

Lord Kilmore was driving in the Park. He stopped beside the walking group and asked Alison if she cared for a turn in his phaeton. Lord Fane frowned.

Alison felt it was noble of Lord Kilmore to show so soon after his rejection that he held no hard feelings.

"Perhaps I am a little more tired than I thought," she said hastily to Lord Fane. "To sit in the carriage for a few minutes will revive me."

At once, gallantly, he helped her up. Lord Kilmore set his splendid bays in motion. Alison wondered whether they, and the high-perch phaeton, had been paid for.

His lordship was looking at her with raised eyebrows. "Tired?" he mocked.

She explained about having walked Midnight already and he laughed.

"A reasonable excuse, then," he conceded. He seemed to have recovered his spirits and he kept her amused in his usual way. When he returned her to her friends a quarter hour later, Fanny and Robert Gilchrist had their heads together, while Neil and Lord Fane looked far from happy with each other's company. They both welcomed Alison eagerly.

Her exertions of the day did not prevent her dancing the night away, though it was a pity Mr. Trevelyan did not attend the ball. She wanted to ask him about the propriety of taking Midnight to Hyde Park, and perhaps to cajole him into driving them there, but he had gone out of Town for a few days.

Aunt Di's ankle improved slowly. Without the advice and transportation Mr. Trevelyan could have provided, Alison continued to walk the dog in the brick fields.

One wet day she put the chore off till late afternoon in the hope that it would stop raining. Lady Emma needed the landau, so the coachman drove off after dropping Alison in Great Ormond Street, to call for her later. Though the drizzle had slackened to a general dampness in the air, she decided when she reached the fields that the ground was too muddy to tramp across. Instead she and Midnight circled round through the streets, going as far east as the Islington Road.

The air was fresh and clean and Alison enjoyed her walk, but it was a long way. She was pleased, when she reached Grays Inn Lane again, to see Lord Kilmore descend from a waiting carriage.

"I came to fetch you," he said, "but when I reached your aunts' house I was told you had not yet returned. I have been driving about looking for you."

"I did not take my usual route because of the rain. I daresay that is why you are not driving your phaeton?"

"I thought you would be more comfortable in a closed carriage in this weather." He handed her in and was attempting to follow when Midnight pushed past him and set both front feet solidly on the carriage floor. Eying him with disfavour, Lord Kilmore brushed at his dampened inexpressibles. "Surely the dog can take himself home!"

"If he was allowed to wander by himself I should not have had to come to walk him," Alison pointed out. "Besides, once he has decided to get in I am not capable of dissuading him, and I rather doubt that you are."

Midnight clambered in with his rear legs and obligingly moved to the centre, sitting down with a thump that shook the carriage. He looked round at Lord Kilmore as if inviting him to join them.

Sighing, his lordship took his place and closed the door. The odour of wet dog filled the air as the carriage jolted into motion. Within a few seconds the windows steamed up, hiding the outside world as if it had ceased to exist. Lord Kilmore raised a handkerchief to his nose.

"Perhaps I had best open a window," suggested Alison.

"Impossible, I fear. I borrowed the carriage from a friend who has an unconscionable dread of draughts. The windows are fastened shut."

Suddenly uneasy, Alison rubbed a clear spot on the glass. The rain-washed street was indistinguishable from a hundred others, but surely they ought to have turned into Guilford Street by now. She had not noticed a left turn.

She was enlarging her peephole when Lord Kilmore reached across Midnight's head and captured her hand in his.

"You will ruin your glove."

Alison pulled her hand free. "This is not the way to Great Ormond Street."

"I am taking you to Park Street."

"Lady Emma would faint if I took Midnight there all wet and muddy. We must take him home first. Tell your coachman to turn round."

Lord Kilmore shook his head. "I'm sorry, but he has orders to go straight on."

"What do you mean?" Her unease deepened. "You are not taking me to Lady Emma's," she accused.

"I had hoped it would take you longer to realize that aught is amiss," he said regretfully.

"Where are you taking me?"

"Don't be afraid, my dear, I mean you no harm. I had hoped to do the thing properly, but you turned me down and I cannot wait. I am scarce one step ahead of the bailiffs, you see."

"You said you are fond of me." She tried to stop her voice wobbling.

"I am, devilish fond. And you confessed that you like me, did you not? I disagree that we shall not suit." He moved closer.

Midnight dropped his great black head on the seat between them. His lordship moved back.

Heartened, Alison repeated her question. "Where are we going?"

"Why, where do you think, my dear? To Gretna."

PHILIP WAS AWARE THAT recently Alison had withdrawn from him in some indistinct, indefinable fashion. She was no less friendly, no less delightful a companion, but there was a shadow of reserve between them. He had been glad of an excuse to go down to his Buckinghamshire estate for a few days.

Between estate business, his family and sociable neighbours, he was as fully occupied at Nether Beeches as in Town. Usually he preferred country life, but this time he had a nagging sense of something missing. He even looked forward to his return to London.

He set out on a fine morning, driving his curricle. Washed by overnight rain, the fresh green of new beech leaves gleamed in the sun; the hedgerows were busy with nesting birds. His thoughts flew at once at Alison. She had turned a muddy trudge among the sordid brick kilns into a merry outing. What joy she would take in this pastoral scene!

He knew very well that it was Alison who made the difference. It was her enthusiasm that rendered the most tedious ton parties enjoyable. Her pleasure in the company of the most unlikely people had made him look beyond the label "urchin" or "eccentric old maid" to see them as individuals. He was even prepared to credit her influence for his split with the government. She had overturned his useful, placid, but dull life—and all she wanted was a lord for a husband.

It began to rain. The clouds that had watered Buckinghamshire last night were stalled over the London basin. Philip pulled over to the side of the road and helped his groom raise the curricle's hood.

"You'd best come in beside me, John," he said, aware that the idea would not have crossed his mind a few months past.

With the leather apron fastened across their legs they were protected from the worst of the weather. Nonetheless, by the time Philip pulled up in front of his Green Street mansion he was damp and depressed.

At that moment he became aware of three things: the boy who ran to his horses' heads was Squeak; the hack tied to the railing in front of his house was Emma's roan mare; and the gentleman standing at his open front door, apparently arguing with his butler, was Lord Deverill.

Even as Philip extricated himself from the apron's soggy embrace, Neil Deverill turned and ran down the steps.

"Don't get down, Trevelyan!" he cried. "That devil Kilmore has run off with Alison. Another minute and I'd have left without you."

"How do you know? Where has he taken her? I shall have to hitch up another team. John, the bays, fast."

The groom jumped down and disappeared towards the mews at a run.

"I happened to be at Lady Emma's when yon lad brought word." Deverill hitched his thumb towards Squeak, who nodded importantly. "It seems there's always one of them keeping an eye on Alison, but to-day business was bad because of the weather so the three were all tailing her."

"We seen the nob 'tice Miss Alison into 'is rumble an' off they goes, so we all 'ops on be'ind."

Philip swung down to the pavement, to stretch his legs and to interrogate the sodden, shivering urchin. "Which road did they take?"

"'E went norf, guv. Soon as we 'its the Great Norf Road, I drops off, see, an' comes 'ome on anuvver rumble to split to the gentry mort. If they turns off the 'pike, me bruvver'll stop off to mark the way, an' Tarry Joe'll stay wiv 'em. Tarry Joe, 'e don't know *B* from a broomstick, but if you wants to run a rig, 'e's a bloody wonder, 'e is."

"Kilmore is heading north," Deverill translated. "Squeak returned on another carriage to tell Lady Emma. If they turn off the highway, his brother will—"

"Yes, I understand. You'd best be off, Deverill. You're armed? Good. I'll be right behind you." Philip turned to his butler, who had come half-way down the steps. "See that the boy is dried and fed, and send word to Lady Emma that I am gone with Lord Deverill, if you please." He waved farewell to Deverill, who cantered away as half a dozen grooms appeared with Philip's four bays and a four-in-hand harness.

"You want me along, sir?" asked John.

Philip shook his head. "I've a feeling I shall be picking up a pair of tigers somewhere en route. I don't need to tell you to keep a still tongue in your head."

"Mum's the word, sir."

Ten minutes later he was driving north out of London, his hands steady, his mind a raging torrent of fury and fear.

CHAPTER SEVENTEEN

ALISON SURVEYED THE ROOM with distaste. "There are cobwebs in the corners," she said, wrinkling her nose, "and it smells."

Midnight found the smells delectable. He padded around, sniffing in the corners.

"Not as much as your dog does," Lord Kilmore pointed out. "Considering the circumstances, you couldn't expect me to take you to one of the better coaching inns. If those fools had had a change of horses ready as I ordered we need not even have set foot in the place." He set his hat and gloves on the table. "When we are married, you shall live in the lap of luxury, I promise you."

"On my money. I do not want to marry you."

"Perhaps I can persuade you that you will enjoy it, my dear."

Taking her by surprise, for he had made no attempt to touch her in the carriage, he swept her into his arms and pressed a passionate kiss on her lips. For a moment she found the new sensation interesting. Then she decided it was horrid and she struggled, trying to turn her face away.

A familiar weight nudged at her thigh. Lord Kilmore suddenly released her, and stepped back as Midnight pushed his way between them.

Alison backed towards the door, wiping her mouth. "I think he needs to go out," she said, though Midnight just stood there looking at her abductor.

"I'll call the tapster to take him," Lord Kilmore suggested, giving the dog a wide berth as he moved towards her.

Midnight raised his upper lip, just wrinkling it up at the sides to reveal large, yellowish teeth. He did not go so far as to growl.

His lordship stood stock still. "Does he bite?"

"He never has," Alison said with incurable honesty, "but I have never known him to show his teeth like that before, either."

Lord Kilmore ventured another step. A low rumble began, deep in Midnight's throat.

"On the other hand," said Lord Kilmore with a sigh, "perhaps you had best take him yourself. I did not count on your bringing such a large chaperon with you." He sat down and watched with a self-deprecating smile as she slipped through the door, her guardian at her heels.

Alison looked back. "I am sorry to leave you all to pieces, but it really would not do," she said politely. "I hope you will find another heiress soon."

His laughter followed her out to the muddy inn yard. It was a pity, she thought, that she did not want him for a husband. She had been almost resigned until he kissed her, for she did like him well enough, but that unpleasant experience had confirmed her decision that they would not suit.

The carriage stood horseless in a corner of the yard. No doubt the coachman was sinking a heavy wet in the tap room, while the ostler went in search of fresh horses. It had stopped raining, but dusk was creeping in and Alison had no idea how far from London they had driven. Stoically, she turned towards the sagging gate, glad that she was dressed for walking. Midnight padded beside her.

She rested her hand on his head. "Thank you, boy. I'll buy you a big juicy bone."

A piercing whistle made her jump.

"Oy! Miss Alison! Wait!"

Tarry Joe ran towards her, his gait most peculiar as his holey, laceless boots squelched in the mud.

"Good gracious," said Alison, "where did you spring from?"

"Off the back o' the gentry cove's rumble. Let you scarper, did 'e?"

"Midnight persuaded him. I am excessively glad to see you, Joe. How far is it to London?"

The boy shrugged his thin shoulders. "'Ell of a ways," he said philosophically. "Let's get goin' afore 'is nibs changes 'is mind."

The lane was just as muddy as the yard, and they made slow progress between looming hedges. Alison was somewhat cheered when Joe told her that he had sent Squeak to notify Lady Emma of her abduction. Still, it was growing dark and she had precisely eighteen pence in her pocket—not that any respectable hostelry would take her in for a king's ransom in her present condition.

A horseman appeared round a bend in the lane, silhouetted against the deepening blue of the clearing sky.

"Alison?"

"Neil!" Lifting her skirts, she ran towards him, tripped in a pot-hole, landed on hands and knees, was up again and caught in his arms. "Oh Neil!" She burst into tears.

"Faith, you're not going to turn into a watering pot on me?" he said severely.

"N-no, it's just that I am so very glad to see you. I was afraid I should have to walk back to London."

"No fear of that. Trevelyan's just behind me. But where is the devil who stole you away? I've a bone to pick with the spalpeen."

"He is back that way at a horrid little alehouse. Leave him be, Neil. He did not harm me. He just wanted to marry me."

"And I just want to tap his claret! Come on, cousin, you can ride behind me."

"I am *not* going back to that place, Neil Deverill. I want to go home."

"We can't ride double so far on Lady Emma's mare anyway. Best keep walking till you meet Trevelyan." Without further ado her cousin swung up onto his mount, saluted her with a wave and cantered on down the lane.

"Werl, if that don't beat old 'Arry!" remarked Tarry Joe admiringly. "Rarin' fer a mill, 'e is."

"How *could* he!" stormed Alison, glaring after her cousin with muddy hands on hips. "This is the outside of enough. I shall never speak to him again. Should we go on or back?"

"There's a sorta wooden step in these 'ere bushes." The child of city streets indicated the hedgerow. "You c'd set there an' wait fer Mr. Trevelyan."

"A stile? But supposing he does not come."

"Now there's a nob wot if 'e says 'e's acomin' you c'n put yer last farthin' on it, Miss Alison. You set yourself down comfy-like wiv ol' Midnight an' I'll 'op along an' make sure Bubble don't miss 'im at the turn-orf."

Deserted by all her rescuers but one, Alison sat down on the stile and watched the small figure tramp off, patient and tireless, in the gathering gloom.

"Oh, Midnight," she sighed, "men are all quite impossible. Thank heaven for dogs."

He laid his great head in her lap and looked up at her worshipfully.

The evening star was twinkling in the west but no others had yet joined it when Alison heard Tarry Joe's voice again. "Jus' roun' this bend, guv." A pair of weary horses appeared, and two more, and the shadowy mass of a curricle. As it stopped beside her, Alison stood up and curtsied.

"Good evening, sir. What a pleasant surprise to meet you here tonight."

With a crack of laughter Philip jumped down and bowed, an elegant, sweeping bow fit for a cavalier. "Good evening, ma'am. I trust I see you well?"

"As well as can be expected. I am very tired, Philip, and I want to go home, but I daresay we ought to go and see if Neil is come to any harm. Or if he has killed poor Lord Kilmore," she added.

"*Poor* Lord Kilmore?" he queried, taking her hand and helping her up into the carriage with an arm about her waist.

His warm clasp, his steady strength, were unutterably comforting, but Alison drew away from him a little as he joined her and urged his team onward. She must not forget that he loved Lady Emma.

"*Poor* Lord Kilmore," she repeated. "It was very wicked in him to abduct me, to be sure, but no harm has come of it and he is left without a feather to fly. And Neil is very angry."

"I confess to having more sympathy for Neil than for Kilmore. I also am very angry."

"I hope you do not mean to hit him too! Perhaps we had best go straight home and leave Neil to look after himself."

Philip laughed softly. "You do not know the meaning of the word vengeance, do you?"

"Of course I do, but I cannot see any point in it. Besides, Lord Kilmore is my friend, and one does not cast off a friend because he makes one mistake. If he was truly evil he could have shot Midnight, or run him through with a sword or something."

"If Kilmore has been brandishing a pistol we must certainly check on Deverill's safety."

"He did *not* brandish a pistol. I told you, he is not a real villain at all, or he would have had a rapier and perhaps a dagger. He would have hit me on the head and chained me in a dungeon, or imprisoned me in a high tower remote from the world. And Neil did not behave in the least like a proper hero, either, leaving me beside the road like that!" Her vexation revived. "Midnight was splendid, though."

"So Joe told me. I shall have to do something for those boys."

The muttered conversation on the box behind them ceased abruptly.

"The first thing is to find them dry clothes," Alison said. "I know they do not seem to notice discomfort, but they are both soaked to the skin."

"Practicality is not the least of your virtues. Ah, this must be the place." He drove into the yard. "Well, one thing is certain, I'll not leave my cattle here overnight!"

In exchange for a couple of guineas the slatternly landlady promised to provide dry togs for Bubble and Tarry Joe. She seemed unperturbed by the goings-on in her inn. Alison was glad she had not appealed to the woman for help.

Philip preceded Alison into the room from which Midnight had rescued her, then stood back to allow her to enter.

Despite her lack of desire for vengeance, she was incensed to find Neil sitting at the table with Lord Kilmore, drinking brandy. Then she noticed that the latter winced when he rose upon her entrance, and that one of his eyes was rapidly swelling shut. She hoped Philip would consider honour satisfied.

Philip was surveying the pair with approval, but Neil was regarding Alison with distinct disapproval.

"So that's where the mud came from!" He brushed at his coat.

She looked down. Both cloak and skirt were caked with mud to well above the knee, and her gloves were filthy. "You saw me fall," she began indignantly, but on a plaintive note added, "however I am too tired to argue about it now. I wish someone will take me home."

"Just a few minutes more." Philip drew out a chair for her at the table. "Deverill, a word with you."

He and Neil went to stand by the empty grate. Alison sat down and pulled off her gloves. Lord Kilmore pushed his across the table to her.

"Wear these." His smile was crooked. "I'm sorry, it was a stupid idea."

"I'm sorry Neil hit you. I told him not to. Will you be all right?"

"The people here know me. I shall come about."

Alison felt in her pocket. The coins had not fallen out when she tripped. She put them on the table, a shilling and two threepenny bits. "Here, it is not much but it's all I have on me. I wish... I wish I might have fallen in love with you." Red-faced, she jumped up and went over to Philip and Neil.

"I'll not take a reward for rescuing me own cousin!"

"Call it payment for favours received."

"Oho, so that's the way of it, is it now? I've had me suspicions."

Neil's look of enlightenment and Philip's warning glance puzzled Alison. She decided to ignore them in favour of doing her cousin a good turn.

"You must not stand on your pride, Neil. Think of Bridey." She turned to Philip. "Neil wants to marry his Irish sweetheart, sir, and emigrate to the colonies."

It was Philip's turn to look enlightened, and oddly relieved. "That should not be difficult," he said. "Would a government post in Canada suit you? I'll have a word with Castlereagh. As a fellow Irishman, he will doubtless be glad to oblige. And for your Bridey's sake you'll accept something to set you up comfortably."

Neil's truculent expression was fading. "I'll take the position and a loan, sir, and thank you for it."

Philip nodded. "Come to my house tomorrow and we shall work out the details. Now we had best be on our way, for poor Emma and the aunts must be in high fidgets by now. I'd take you up, Deverill, but between the dog and the boys we'll not have an inch to spare. I'll be leaving my team at the Eight Bells in Hatfield, so I shall arrange a change of mount for you, and for Emma's mare to be brought on tomorrow."

He smiled at Alison. As she took his arm, she recalled Lady Emma's description of the man she wanted to marry: "Someone who solves problems." Philip had everything under control. All she had to do was to climb into the curricle and lean back wearily against the squabs, knowing that he would take care of her.

He drove for some minutes in silence, then said abruptly, "I feel that Kilmore got off much too lightly. He really did not harm you?"

"He did kiss me. It was horrid. I cannot imagine why any lady should want to be kissed, but some do, do they not?"

"Yes, indeed."

She heard amusement in his voice, "*That* sort of female," she said, feeling very worldly-wise. But it was not a proper subject of conversation with a gentleman, even with Philip. Especially with Philip, for she could not help wondering what it would be like if *he* kissed her, though she knew he loved Lady Emma. "Thank you for helping Neil. Will Lord Castlereagh really find him a position?"

"If I ask him at once, before he discovers I mean to defect from the party."

"I shall pay you back whatever you give Neil. Surely Aunt Zenobia will not object to advancing the money to me."

His hand covered hers, warm even through the outsize glove she wore. "That will not be necessary. I believe your cousin will repay me in time, and if he does not I am well able to stand the nonsense, you know."

"Lady Edgehill said something about you being wealthy. I did not pay much heed at the time."

"Rich enough to buy an abbey, if I wanted one."

"It would be prodigious romantic to live in an abbey." She sighed. "But sadly uncomfortable, I daresay. Sometimes I think that everything Mrs. Meeke and Mrs. Cuthbertson ever wrote is all a hum."

"You are burned to the socket. Everything will look brighter in the morning." Philip sounded downright cheerful.

Alison laughed. "That is just what my aunts always used to say. And they were right."

"Of course. Sensible women, your aunts."

Refreshed by their brief rest at the alehouse, the bays soon trotted into the yard of the Eight Bells. Alison stayed in the carriage while Philip made arrangements to stable them and hire a fresh team. Plodding under Neil's unaccustomed weight, Lady Emma's mare carried him in a short while later and he strolled up to the curricle.

"All right?" he asked.

"Yes." She smiled drowsily. "I'm glad about Bridey."

"You're a fine plucky lass, Alison, and it's proud I am to call you cousin. I'll see you in the morning."

"Afternoon," she contradicted. "I shall not wake at least until midday." She gave a huge yawn.

Philip rejoined her and they set off again. On the smooth, newly macadamized road, the well-sprung carriage rocked her gently. She felt herself slipping sideways, coming to rest with her cheek against Philip's shoulder, but it was too much effort to move. She slept.

CHAPTER EIGHTEEN

PHILIP LOOKED UP as Emma came into the drawing-room. Presuming on long friendship, he did not rise but saluted her with his glass of brandy.

"The poor child hardly stirred as Carter and I put her to bed." Emma poured herself a glass of canary and took a seat on the opposite side of the hearth, where a small fire burned more for comfort than for warmth.

"I can imagine how she feels. I am exhausted and I did not go through a quarter of what she suffered."

"I am weary myself. I cannot think how I should have survived the anxiety without Mr. Osborne's kindness."

"He was here to hold your hand, I collect."

She flushed. "Yes, he was. As Alison's guardian, in a sense, he had to be told, and I asked him to stay with me until you brought her home. I have a great regard for Ral...Mr. Osborne."

"I don't mean to tease, Emma, but it is something more than regard, is it not? Forgive me if I am wrong, I would say you are heels over head in love."

"No, not heels over head. That was how I felt about Stephen—lost in a romantic haze, unable to think straight let alone see past the end of my nose. My feeling for Ralph is very different. I am so happy with him, but I am willing to acknowledge that he has one or two faults—very small faults!—such as thinking he is always right."

"Which is common to all the male sex. A small fault, to be sure, and one easily remedied by any female with the least ingenuity. But do you also see his great disadvantage?"

"His birth. His being in trade. If I could not see it for myself, my family would have made sure to point it out," she said bitterly. "I have not even confessed yet that I mean to marry Ralph, yet already Mama has deplored my friendship with him and Papa has warned me not to ask him to put Ralph up for any clubs. I dread to think what they will say if I tell them that we are to be wed. I believe they would refuse to attend the wedding, and I could not bear to humiliate Ralph so."

"You do not owe your family anything. This is the moment when all your years of stubborn independence bear fruit. If you think they will refuse an invitation, then do not invite them." Philip enjoyed her stare of surprise.

"I was certain you would agree with them! If anyone believes in pride of birth, it is you."

"Alison has taught me the error of my ways. I am ready to admit to being heels over head in love."

"You! With Alison?" Emma was astonished now. "She is pretty and amiable—indeed, as I have told her, she is the pleasantest of all my protégées. But you have had any number of diamonds of the first water flung at your head over the years."

"Any number," he agreed. "Alison, on the other hand, is unique."

"What of the aunts?"

"There are eccentrics in the best families."

"Not generally in such profusion."

"Perhaps not, but then I am rather fond of them. They are not at all vulgar, except perhaps for Mrs. Winkle, and to her I must be grateful for the opportunity of knowing Alison. I shall encourage Mrs. Winkle to settle in Cheltenham with Mrs. Colonel What's-her-name, which will be a great relief to the others, I have no doubt."

"And those ragamuffins she is so friendly with?"

"Those ragamuffins saved her today. Tarry Joe wants to be a sailor, and Bubble a groom, and Squeak I believe would profit from going to school. I see no difficulty there."

"You sound as if you are on intimate terms with them!"

"I am. I have also accepted responsibility for Neil Deverill and his Bridey, and I am even prepared to take on Midnight, who also had a hand—paw?—in the rescue."

"The Newfoundland? Bridey? No, do not tell me; no doubt I shall hear everything in the morning."

"You see, I am ready for anything. The only trouble is that Alison regards me as an uncle. A favourite uncle, I hope, but nonetheless an uncle."

"I do not believe she does. She has told me with unnecessary firmness that she looks upon Ralph as an uncle, yet she never said anything of the sort about you."

"As a friend, then. That is a little better."

"I fear I cannot hold out much hope. She is so very determined to wed a lord."

"Yet she turned down Kilmore." Philip refused to give up hope.

"A gazetted fortune hunter. She will not reject Fane if he can bring himself to overlook her breeding."

"No, she will not reject Fane. It would be easy to put a spoke in that wheel, but if she wants him and can win him, she shall have him." He sighed. "She gave every last penny in her pocket to Kilmore, you know," he added irrelevantly. "A shilling or two."

"To Kilmore! I will give you this, Philip, Alison is unique."

He drove home with a wry smile on his lips. Perhaps he was a fool, but he could not forget that Alison was beginning to grow disillusioned with the works of Mrs. Cuthbertson and Mrs. Meeke.

THE SEASON WAS DRAWING to a close. There was a frantic flurry of balls and picnics and breakfasts as mamas of daughters who had not yet won a prize in the Matrimonial Stakes made a last-minute bid for a trophy.

Not all parties had that purpose, however. Lord and Lady Witherington planned an intimate soirée to celebrate Fanny's betrothal to Mr. Robert Gilchrist. As a member of Robert's family, Lady Emma was naturally included, and as her protégée and Fanny's best friend, Alison was also invited.

Fanny delivered the invitation herself. It was a fine morning, so the two girls went for a stroll around Grosvenor Square, followed at a discreet distance by Fanny's maid.

"You will come, will you not?" Fanny begged. "It was through you I met Robert."

"Yes, of course. I would cancel a dozen other engagements if necessary. You really love him?" Alison tried not to sound sceptical, but she had a tendency to see Robert through the eyes of his elder sister.

"You are thinking that he is not in the least like the hero of a novel," said her friend accurately. "You are right, but he is such a dear. I am always comfortable with him, and that is a great deal, is it not? I dare say it would be monstrous uncomfortable to live with the hero of a gothick romance."

"Perhaps." Alison could not deny that that thought had crossed her mind more than once.

"I persuaded Mama to ask Lord Fane," Fanny added with a giggle. "With any luck our engagement will set him thinking in the right direction."

"As long as he does not suppose that I had any hand in the invitation!"

"He is some sort of distant connexion of the Gilchrists, I collect, so it is quite reasonable to invite him. It is time you made a push to attach him, Alison, or he will never make up his mind to offer. I would not tell this to anyone else, but I practically had to pro-pose to Robert. Otherwise the poor dear would have gone on casting sheep's eyes at me over his flute for-ever."

"I *will* not set my cap at Lord Fane. The cases are quite different."

"He seems to blow now hot, now cold. It is a pity that your cousin and Lord Kilmore are both gone. The competition spurred him on."

"I miss Neil. And Lord Kilmore, too, as a matter of fact. You do not suppose Lord Fane heard about that business?" Alison had told Fanny all about the ab-duction.

"If word had got out I am sure someone would have whispered in my ear by now."

"All the same, he did not at all like my walking Midnight. Any reminder of my family discomposes him sadly."

"In a way that is good," Fanny consoled her. "When he does pop the question you will know that he must be deeply in love with you to overcome his qualms. To win against obstacles is far more romantic. It is most vexatious that no one had the least objection to Robert and I becoming betrothed."

Her doleful face made Alison laugh.

Fanny's plan appeared to have the desired effect. Throughout the soirée Lord Fane hovered solicitously over Alison, making remarks about the felicity of the married state. At the end of the evening, as he tenderly placed her wrap about her shoulders, he said with a look of marked significance, "May I have the pleasure of calling on you tomorrow morning, Miss Larkin? I have something most particular to say to you."

"Lady Emma and I will be delighted to receive you, as always, my lord," she answered primly, and received a nod of approval.

In the carriage going home she told Lady Emma, who agreed that it sounded as if his lordship was ready to declare himself. In a flutter of euphoria mingled with apprehension amounting almost to dread, Alison lay long awake that night.

Philip turned up at the breakfast table the next morning. His news almost drove Lord Fane from Alison's mind.

"I've found a berth as cabin boy for Tarry Joe," he announced. "Bubble went to work in the mews yesterday, and already I have a good report of his way with horses from John. Squeak starts school tomorrow."

Alison flew round the table and planted a kiss on his cheek, then looked guiltily at Lady Emma. "I know you said I must not do that, but you did say also that it was not quite scandalous with Phil...Mr. Trevelyan. Because he is such a good friend of yours."

Lady Emma sighed and shook her head. Philip, his colour heightened, looked as if he was trying not to smile. Alison returned to her seat. There was a curious burning sensation in her lips and she toyed with her food, losing interest in it. Perhaps kissing would not be so horrid after all, with the right person.

"I take it you approve," Philip said.

"It is splendid of you, especially to arrange what each wants most, not what you think best for them."

They were still in the breakfast parlour when Lord Fane was announced, at an unheard-of hour for that most proper of gentleman.

"Off you go, Alison," Lady Emma directed. "I shall join you in fifteen minutes."

The last thing Alison saw as she left the room was Philip's sudden frown as he looked enquiringly at Lady Emma. She felt rushed, propelled into a situation over which she had no control, with no time to consider beforehand. Henry's wink as he ushered her into the drawing-room did not help her composure.

Lord Fane appeared equally nervous. He was pacing up and down with a large bouquet of fully open roses in his hand. The flowers reminded Alison of the boys, and she seized on the topic with relief. Greetings exchanged, bouquet presented and admired, she impulsively reported Mr. Trevelyan's charitable provision for Tarry Joe and Bubble and Squeak.

"Bubble and Squeak!" Lord Fane had so far managed to ignore his beloved's propensity for consorting with guttersnipes. "It is estimable of Trevelyan to be sure, but I could wish you were not on terms of such familiarity with...with such oddly named characters," he ended lamely.

Alison recognized that she had blotted her copybook. Instead of the expected dismay, she felt she had had a narrow escape. She was not quite ready to receive a proposal from Lord Fane, long though she had hoped for it. When he invited her to drive in the Park that afternoon she accepted cheerfully. He was taking his leave as Lady Emma came in.

"Going so soon, my lord?" she enquired.

He flushed, mumbled something and hurried out.

Alison did not tell Lady Emma that she had shocked him with talk of the boys. "He simply failed to screw his courage to the sticking point," she reported.

"YOU WERE SO CERTAIN he would ask her this morning." Philip slowed his chestnuts as they turned into Rotten Row. Emma had never wondered why he called them Spaniard and Conqueror. "What went wrong?"

Hyde Park was at its best. The trees were dressed in spring green and the birds were shouting loud enough to be heard over the clop of hooves, the creak of wheels and murmur of voices. The sun shone on the magnificent spectacle of half the ton taking the air. Only this morning, on Lord Fane's arrival, the world had suddenly turned drab and grey; now it showed itself to Philip in its true colours again—a delightful place to be.

Emma shrugged her shoulders. "She said only that he failed to screw his courage to the sticking point."

"That is the sort of remark that makes me love her," Philip said, laughing. "She was not greatly distressed, then?"

"For all she is so open it is not always easy to tell how she feels, but I think not."

"Are you sure she understands how little time she has left? If Fane retires to the country without speaking first, she may never see hide nor hair of him again."

They were interrupted at that moment by Lady Edgehill, whose barouche drew up alongside the tilbury.

"Emma, my dear, that bonnet becomes you delightfully."

"Thank you, Mama."

"Do you not agree, Philip? Our dear girl is in looks today. There is nothing like an amiable companion to bring out a young lady's best looks."

"Emma is never less than handsome, Lady Edgehill." From the corner of his eyes, Philip saw Emma's fulminating expression. He added hastily, "We are blocking the way, ma'am. Excuse us, pray."

"It is a wonder," snorted Emma as they drove on, "that she has not yet egged Papa on to ask your intentions. It would not surprise me to learn that they are encouraging you to run off with me to Gretna Green."

"Lord no, your mother would never countenance such indecorum, even to see the knot safely tied."

"Why will they not accept Ralph?" she wailed.

Philip was astonished at such an outburst from his usually imperturbable friend.

"Hush!" he hissed. "Lady Jersey's carriage is upon us. Compose yourself and smile. I have an idea—no, better than that, I have a famous notion."

"What is it?" she asked eagerly, bowing and smiling at Lady Jersey.

"I shall have a house party at Nether Beeches. It will serve to give Alison one last chance with Fane."

"That is excessively noble of you, Philip, but—"

"You will come, of course, and I shall invite Osborne. After that, it is up to the two of you."

"Philip, you angel!"

Much to his embarrassment she kissed him heartily on the cheek, just as Lord Fane's carriage came into view. Alison's wave of greeting faltered.

"Damn," muttered Philip through gritted teeth.

CHAPTER NINETEEN

GOLDEN GREEN LIGHT and shadow flickered among
the smooth grey beech trunks. Alison exclaimed in delight as a rust-red squirrel bounded across the road and
sat with bushy tail erect to watch the Edgehills' carriage roll by. Lady Emma and Fanny exchanged toler-
ant glances.

They emerged into sunshine again. Parkland dotted
with mighty oaks and chestnuts, browsed by a herd of
fallow deer, swept up to a mansion of age-mellowed red
brick. It stood two-thirds of the way up the slope,
sheltered from the north by the crest of the hill, gazing
with an air of benevolence over the valley.

Alison gasped. "Is that Nether Beeches?"

"It is." Emma was amused.

"I never imagined anything half so grand. Mr.
Trevelyan is a very important gentleman, is he not?"

"His wealth, his family connexions and his personal qualities have brought him influence and au-
thority, both here and in Town, that many a peer might
envy. Yes, he is a gentleman of considerable consequence."

"Papa says he is a pillar of the establishment,"
Fanny put in.

"I did not know. He is not at all pretentious. He
never talks about the distinguished history of the
Trevelyans, only about his family, his brothers and

sisters. They sound most agreeable. I hope I shall meet them?''

"Mark is the vicar of the parish, and Dorothy is to be his hostess, I collect."

"Lady Vernon? She has a daughter and two sons, does she not? Do you think they will be here, too?''

"You seem to know all there is to know about the family! It is not at all like Philip to bore his acquaintances with such stuff."

"But I was not bored. I never had parents and brothers and sisters, so hearing about them was almost like a fairy tale. I do hope Lady Vernon's children will be here."

Mr. Osborne, who with Robert Gilchrist was escorting them on horseback, drew closer to the carriage window and addressed Lady Emma.

"I did not expect so impressive a mansion."

Alison thought he sounded anxious, dismayed even, and she felt a sudden sympathy for him. They were both embarking upon uncharted seas. Lady Emma seemed to understand, for she spoke reassuringly.

"I came here often as a child. As I told you, my father's house, which is now my eldest brother's, lies not two miles off. You will find Nether Beeches perfectly homely and comfortable. Philip does not go in for pomp and display."

Mr. Osborne smiled at her warmly and drew off a little. He was a splendid figure on horseback, holding himself erect but with an easy dignity Alison had to admire. Nonetheless she did not want to marry him. A moment of panic shook her—she might end up doing just that if Lord Fane did not come up to scratch in the next two weeks.

Philip came down the front steps to meet them. Alison expected to be a little in awe of the owner of this magnificent estate. However, he was no less approachable in buckskins, top boots and a slightly worn shooting jacket than in impeccable evening dress. As he ushered the party into his house, she asked him eagerly whether the deer were tame enough to be fed by hand and whether his sister had brought her children to Nether Beeches.

"You may ask her yourself," he said, smiling. "Dorothy, you know Emma, of course. These beautiful young ladies are Miss Fanny Witherington and Miss Alison Larkin."

Dorothy, Lady Vernon, was a plump, cheerful matron two or three years younger than her brother. She welcomed his guests warmly, and said to Alison, "I left my little imps at home, but I mean to go over now and then to see that they have not driven their governess to distraction. It is not far. Perhaps you will like to go with me?"

"Yes, please." Alison accepted with such alacrity that Lady Vernon laughed.

"Good. I daresay Philip will drive us." She cast a sly glance at her brother. "Their father is only too glad of a respite. Ah, Jenny, there you are. Come and make the acquaintance of our guests."

Her ladyship looked toward a tall, quiet, fair-haired girl who turned out to be the Reverend Mark Trevelyan's betrothed. Alison envied her for belonging to the family.

"Shall I take Miss Witherington and Miss Larkin to their chambers, ma'am?" she enquired in a soft voice.

"Yes, please do, Jenny, but how many times have I told you to call me Dorothy! Philip, you will see to

Robert and Mr. Osborne, will you not, so that I can make Emma comfortable. Miss Witherington, your parents are expected to arrive in time to dine with us, I collect?''

"Yes, ma'am," Fanny agreed. "Papa had some last minute business in Town."

"And Lord Fane will be here tomorrow morning. What a delightful party we shall have, Philip." Lady Vernon beamed with pleasure and bustled up the stairs like a mother goose leading her goslings.

Alison saw Fanny exchange a few words with Robert on the landing before they followed Miss Jenny Barton to a pair of prettily decorated chambers with a connecting door. She was not at all surprised when, after tidying herself quickly, Fanny disappeared.

"She is betrothed to Mr. Gilchrist," Alison explained to Jenny. "Tell me all about Mr. Mark Trevelyan." She sat down in a well-cushioned window-seat, from which she could see Fanny and Robert strolling with unconvincing casualness towards a shrubbery.

Jenny's shyness was not proof against such an invitation. She described how they had met and catalogued in glowing terms the young vicar's many virtues. Not given to scepticism in the first place, Alison was the more ready to believe him a saint because Philip had told her much the same. By the time they went downstairs to take tea, the girls were well on the way to being intimate friends.

After tea, most of the party went out into the gardens. The sun still shone high in a flawless blue sky, the long June evening scarcely begun. Alison found herself wandering through a rose garden with Philip.

"How Aunt Polly would love this," she said, burying her nose in a gloriously fragrant, deep red bloom. "Nothing grows so well in London."

"If you think they would enjoy it, I should like to invite all your aunts to come down for a few days later in the summer."

She glanced back dubiously at the grand mansion behind them. "That is very kind of you, sir, but I am afraid they would feel lost in your house."

"There is a cottage not half a mile off that I use for guests who prefer privacy. They could stay there. I shall ask them when we return to Town. Only think how happy Midnight and the terriers would be."

"*Aux anges!* You mean to invite them, too?" Alison laughed—and wondered whether she would be included in the invitation. At least it meant that she might see him again, even when she was no longer living with Lady Emma. "Aunt Di will certainly accept, then."

They strolled on into the formal Italian garden and joined the others.

Alison met Mark Trevelyan at dinner that evening. Though taller and more slender, he looked very like his brother. That, together with his gentle manners and obvious adoration of Jenny, endeared him to Alison at once. She was equally ready to like Dorothy's husband, Sir Alfred Vernon, though he showed a distinct tendency to ignore her as soon as he discovered that she did not ride. His chief interests appeared to revolve around hunting, coursing and shooting.

When the ladies retired to the drawing-room after dinner, leaving the gentlemen to their port and brandy, Alison told Jenny how much she liked the vicar. Fanny began to sing Robert's praises, and as the talk continued, Alison could not help feeling somewhat left out, especially when the two young gentlemen came in very soon, without their elders. Not that she was by any means excluded from the conversation, but it seemed an age before the others joined them.

Lord Witherington looked somewhat out of temper, and Philip wryly amused. Alison seized the first opportunity to ask Philip what was amiss.

"I have ruffled his lordship's feathers," he confessed. "He thought he was to be entertained by a true blue Tory. We had something of a political discussion over the port and he found out he was mistaken."

"Oh dear, did you tell him you are turning Whig? Fanny said he called you a pillar of the establishment."

"Lord, did he really?" Philip groaned, laughing. "His pillar has crumbled; that is why he is so shocked."

"He will not make Fanny leave?"

"That would be unpardonably rude, even to a Whig. No, you need not fear losing your friend's company."

"I am glad, even though I do think Jenny will be my friend, too."

"You have a happy knack of making friends, my dear. Go and work your wiles on Lord Witherington for me."

He watched as she obeyed, and soon had the felicity of seeing his lordship's face lose its frown.

When all their guests had at last retired, Philip and his sister mounted the stairs together.

"Alison is a dear," said Dorothy, patting his arm. "I do not wonder that you are madly in love with her."

"I'm glad you like her, but it would have made no difference to me if you had not."

"Of course not. What passes my understanding is that you have invited Lord Fane to come down here."

"It is not pure altruism, I assure you. I could not bear to marry her and then find that she was pining after a title."

"I cannot believe she is so set on marrying a lord. I never saw a less calculating creature in my life."

"She is beginning to grow out of that youthful romanticism." Philip's smile was tender, yet he sighed. "In a way it is a pity."

"You are taking a fearful risk of losing her."

"I know it. But what else can I do?" The question was rhetorical. He kissed his sister's cheek and went off to bed, wondering if he had completely lost his wits to invite his rival into his own home.

ALISON, USED TO SLEEPING through street cries and rumbling wagons, was awakened early next morning by the song of a thrush. The liquid, warbling notes tugged her out of bed. Barefooted, she ran to the open window to see a plain brown bird with a speckled breast flutter down from a branch to the dew-drenched lawn and begin a tug-of-war with a worm.

The sun was burning off the last wisps of morning mist. The outside world was so fresh and inviting that Alison could not resist. She scrambled into a morning gown and ran downstairs.

In the hall she paused, wondering which way to go. At that moment a maid pushed open the door to the servants' quarters, and the lure of the gardens was overpowered by a heavenly aroma. Alison followed her nose. A few minutes later she was seated at the table in a huge, airy kitchen hung with gleaming copper pans, munching a chunk of new-baked bread slathered with creamy butter. The cook, beaming, made a pot of tea, while the housekeeper showed Alison Lady Vernon's menus for the day and explained the problems involved in provisioning a house party.

They were discussing the differences between marketing in Town and in the country when Philip came in, grinning. With a hand on the housekeeper's shoulder he stopped her jumping up, and said to the cook, "Any old bread to spare? Miss Larkin wishes to feed the deer."

Alison carrying a stale loaf, Philip with his mouth full of fresh bread and butter, they went off to find the herd.

By the time Lord Fane arrived at midday, Alison had decided that the country was quite the most delightful place to be. She told him so, when he joined the rest of the party for a cold collation. He responded with a paean of praise for Fane Hall, in which the ornamental lake figured largely.

"Nether Beeches has no ornamental lake," he pointed out. "And peacocks—I believe Trevelyan has no peacocks?"

It was most promising.

With the happy examples of Fanny and Robert, Jenny and Mark before him, his lordship's ardour increased noticeably. The second evening, when everyone strolled out into the twilight gardens after dinner, Alison was not surprised to find herself steered apart from the others.

"I am persuaded you have not visited the jasmine bower at this time of day, Miss Larkin," Lord Fane said hopefully. "The fragrance is at its best now."

Nothing could have been more romantic than to wander among sweet-scented flowers on the arm of an enamoured gentleman while the light faded from the indigo sky. Alison took a seat in the jasmine bower with a sense of rising excitement. The gentleman dropped to one knee in the approved fashion.

"Miss Larkin! Alison, if I may be so bold." He took her hand.

"My lord!" Ah, there was the thrilling tone she had tried for with Lord Kilmore. Lord Fane looked somewhat alarmed.

"Miss Alison, you must know how much I admire, nay, adore you. Since first I met you, my heart has not been my own. I long to call you mine. Give me hope— say, oh say that you will be my bride and my heart shall be yours forever more."

As a speech his declaration was satisfactory, though Alison suspected that it had been lifted from a melodrama and much rehearsed. It was a pity that there was a spider swinging from a gossamer thread not a foot above his lordship's head. Should she warn him? The jasmine fragrance was becoming overpowering and she had a sudden urge to sneeze. Valiantly she suppressed it. It would not do to sneeze in the face of a gentleman making a proposal of marriage.

She became aware that he was awaiting an answer. Her acceptance was on the tip of her tongue when she realized that she did not know his Christian name.

"You hesitate—I have taken you by surprise. Such maidenly modesty does you credit. Allow me to enumerate the advantages that must accrue to you as my wife."

Narrowly missing the spider, he stood up and sat beside her on the stone slab bench, which was growing colder and harder by the minute. She must tell Philip to exchange it for a wooden seat.

Philip! His name was a talisman that opened the door to understanding. How could she wed the man at her side, whose meaningless babble of dignity and consequence flowed past her uncomprehended, when it was Philip she loved.

"I'm sorry," she interrupted, "I cannot marry you."

He patted her hand. "You are afraid that you will not be worthy of your new station in life. It is perfectly understandable. I assure you I have not taken this step without much serious consideration, and I have reached the conclusion that with my assistance you will be able to overcome a slight tendency towards levity. Nor need anyone know about your unfortunate connexions. Naturally I shall not forbid your calling on them now and then when we are in Town, in an unmarked carriage, of course. I know you are much attached to your aunts. Such family sentiment does you no harm in my eyes, I promise you."

"Thank you, my lord, but truly I cannot be your wife."

"Ah well, I shall not press you now. Perhaps you will like to talk to Lady Emma about my offer. She is a sensible woman and will doubtless reassure you as to your fitness for so daunting a position. Every young lady likes to be courted, I know, and it is a woman's privilege to change her mind. I do not despair. Shall we return to the house?"

He rose. Barely visible in the gathering dark, the persistent spider landed on his cheek, ran across his nose and spun down to his lapel. Alison dissolved in a fit of the giggles.

Lord Fane was seriously affronted. It was beneath his dignity to abandon her, but his voice was frosty as he pointed out a step in the path and he did not offer his arm.

Everyone else had gone in. Though Alison wanted to retire to her chamber, and she suspected Lord Fane was equally desirous of avoiding company, they went to the drawing-room. The first sight that met her eyes was Philip and Lady Emma, tête-à-tête on a love-seat, absorbed in low-voiced conversation.

Alison found her work-bag and Lord Fane, with conscious graciousness, brought a branch of candles to the table beside her. She was glad to bow her head over her needlework. Doubtless bent on hiding his discomfiture, he stayed by her, occasionally uttering a commonplace remark which she did not feel it necessary to answer. Never had she suffered through an evening so endless and so painful.

She did not waste a moment on wondering whether his lordship's outrage would last. It was not important. All her energy must go into hiding from Lady Emma and Philip the fact that she loved him.

CHAPTER TWENTY

PHILIP WAS STANDING AT the library window watching Lord Fane's carriage depart down the hill when Dorothy joined him.

"Well?" she demanded.

"A plausible but transparent emergency." Philip's attempt to keep a triumphant grin from his face was not entirely successful. "Have you seen Alison this morning?"

"Not yet. I'd give a good deal to know what she did last night to make him hedge off. All the signs pointed to your defeat."

"They did, did they not? All that was lacking was a full moon. I expect she laughed at the wrong moment. His lordship deplores frivolity in a female."

"I should not call her frivolous; she has a serious side to her. The servants all worship her, you know, and they are better judges of character than anyone. Few young ladies could keep their respect after breakfasting in the kitchen! Do you mean to declare yourself today?"

His fond smile faded. "I think not. The poor child must be sadly disappointed at Fane's defection and she will need time to recover. I shall do what I can to drive off the blue devils. I wonder if she would like to learn to ride?"

"Ask her."

Philip took his sister's advice and was rewarded by the instant brightening of Alison's unwontedly doleful face.

"I should love to! Will you teach me? Or no, I expect there is an aged family retainer who taught you when you were a boy."

"Is that how Mrs. Meeke would have it?"

"Yes, I do not know how many aged retainers she has created. Is she wrong about that, too?"

"By no means. However, Davy is ancient rather than merely aged, and he prefers sitting in the sun on a mounting block to walking across the stable yard. I could find the second oldest groom for you."

"Now you are roasting me. I should much prefer you to teach me, if it will not be a great deal of trouble."

"That depends on how well you follow my directions. Any disobedience and I shall turn you over to the oldest groom."

Her chuckle warmed his heart.

Whether it was due to the threat or not, she proved an apt pupil. By the third day she was ready to venture down to the village to see the improvements to the vicarage that he had set in train in preparation for Mark's marriage. That outing left her stiff, and she was quite happy to ride in his curricle to the Vernons' house to meet his niece and nephews. Fond as he was of the children, it was her joy in playing with them that gave him the most pleasure.

His older sister visited, and gave her approval to his choice.

Time passed, with riding and walking and picnics when the weather was fine, music and games, books and conversation when it rained. A dozen times Philip nearly asked Alison to marry him, but with the sensitivity of a man in love he noticed how now and then she withdrew from him, a sad, pensive expression crossing her elfin face.

He knew he wanted her for his wife even if she did not love him. He tried to be patient. Perhaps on her return to Town, to her aunt's house, she would be willing to look with favour on the suit of an untitled gentleman who loved her very much.

The last day of the house party dawned fair, though a steady westerly wind threatened rain before nightfall. Everyone was up early, and trunks and boxes were despatched London-ward on a loaded fourgon. Alison was to travel with the Witheringtons. She envied Philip his curricle, but while tooling around the country lanes was acceptable, it would not be proper for a young lady to be seen on the high road in a sporting vehicle.

She recalled driving home to London with him after she was abducted by poor Lord Kilmore. It had not seemed to matter then, for a brief time, that he loved Lady Emma.

Even the possibility of returning at a later date with her aunts could not cheer the departure from Nether Beeches. Feeling utterly dejected, she was quite unable to join the chatter as Fanny and her mother discussed bride clothes and wedding plans.

"What colour should you like the bridesmaids' gowns to be, Alison?" Fanny enquired.

Her thoughts far away, Alison started. "Colour? Oh, whatever you choose. Everything should be just as you like it." She shuddered as the horrid notion crossed her mind that Lady Emma might ask her to be a bridesmaid when she married Philip.

When they reached London, the carriage set down the Witheringtons and then carried Alison on to Great Ormond Street. Comforted by a rapturous welcome from her aunts and the dogs, Alison managed to give a lively description of Nether Beeches and the events of her stay. The kitchen was cosy refuge from the rain that now streamed down the windows.

Her trunk arrived just before dinner and was carried up to her chamber. After eating she went up to begin unpacking, a bittersweet task since she knew each garment would remind her of something she had done with Philip while wearing it.

Carter had packed the trunk for her, and for a moment she was afraid Lady Emma's abigail had forgot to give her the key. She found it in her reticule. It turned easily and she lifted the heavy lid.

On top of her clothes lay a white rectangle of paper. Puzzled, she reached for it, letting the lid crash back against the wall. She sat back on her heels, unfolded the sheet, and gasped in shock as she read the few words in Lady Emma's hand.

"Alison, are you all right? Whatever was that great bang?" Aunt Di hurried in.

"Bang? Oh, the lid. Sorry. Aunt Di, I do not know what to do."

"What to do? I knew something was wrong. What is it, dear? What does the letter say?"

Aunt Cleo and Aunt Polly arrived, asking anxiously about the crash. Aunt Di made them sit down and they all looked expectantly at Alison.

She realized how much she loved them. She could never marry anyone who did not accept them as they were. She needed advice, and they knew her better than anyone else in the whole world.

"Lady Emma has eloped with Ralph Osborne," she said.

"Ralph Osborne!" exclaimed Aunt Cleo.

"Oh dear, whatever will Zenobia say?" worried Aunt Polly.

"But you do not care for Mr. Osborne, Alison," Aunt Di pointed out, "so what is upsetting you?"

"Philip—Mr. Trevelyan—loves Lady Emma, and I love Philip!" she wailed.

"Then you ought to be delighted at the news of the elopement." Aunt Di did not seem surprised.

"But I cannot bear to see Philip hurt. He has loved her forever. Do you think if I went to him at once and told him he might be able to catch up with them and bring her back?"

The three spinsters exchanged significant glances.

"But it's raining," protested Aunt Polly.

"All the better," Aunt Di said cryptically. "You must take Midnight, Alison, for you will never find a hackney about here at this hour."

"Do you really think...?" began Aunt Cleo. "Yes, I daresay it will serve. You must wrap up warmly, dear. Is your blue cloak unpacked?"

"Yes, I carried it with me in the carriage. Do you really think I should go? It is not just a silly romantic notion?"

"Consider how unhappy Mr. Trevelyan will be if he finds out too late," Aunt Di reminded her. "And how noble and self-sacrificing he will think you."

Alison was half-way down the street before she realized that Philip would only think her noble and self-sacrificing if he knew that she loved him. She was determined that he should never find out. Huddled in her cloak, she scurried through the steady downpour,

Midnight padding patient and uncomplaining at her side.

By the time she reached Green Street, she was soaked to the skin, her elegant blue cloak a sodden weight on her shoulders. In the past few months she had passed Philip's house dozens of times, but being an unmarried young lady she had never entered within its bachelor portals. Mounting the steps to the pillared and pedimented front door, she nearly cried craven and turned back.

She could not face the walk. Though it was nearly July, she was shivering. Philip would drive her home, even if he laughed at her or was angry at her interference— No, he would not be angry, when she meant well.

She rang the bell.

The butler was not the one she had met at Nether Beeches. His face was wooden as she stammered out her request through chattering teeth.

"P-please, I must see Mr. T-trevelyan."

"The master is not at home."

"B-but I see a light... Oh, you mean he is not receiving. T-tell him Miss Larkin is here. I think he will see me."

The moment he heard her name, his demeanour thawed. "Miss Larkin! Come in, miss, do. Why, you're wet through, miss. Thomas," he addressed a footman, "fetch Mrs. Pugh this instant and tell the master Miss Larkin is come. Allow me to take your cloak, miss." He made shooing motions at Midnight, with the inevitable lack of success.

The footman looked befuddled by the instructions thrown at him. He decided first to stick his head in at the door on the right of the hall, where Alison had seen the light, to announce, "Miss Larkin, sir," before dashing off into the nether regions of the house.

Alison surrendered her cloak to the butler just as Philip came out into the hall. His eyes widened as he caught sight of her and she became aware that her rain-soaked dress clung to every slender curve. The colour rose in her cheeks and she felt hot all over, yet she shivered.

He took her arm, his fingers burning through the thin muslin. "Come in by the fire at once. No, don't tell me anything until you are warm and dry."

"Mrs. Pugh will be here in a moment, sir," the butler assured him.

Philip nodded, but continued to lead her into the room, which was lined with floor to ceiling book shelves. He pushed a chair close to the fire. Following, Midnight slumped on the hearth rug.

"I cannot sit down," Alison protested. "I shall ruin your chair."

He grinned at her, his brown eyes that she had once thought so cold brimming with amusement. "Then drink this." He poured a glass of wine from a decanter on a small, spindly table and handed it to her. "No doubt Mrs. Pugh will bear you off any moment anyway."

"But I must..."

"Drink," he ordered sternly, and she obeyed. The wine was light and slightly sweet. It spread a glow of warmth throughout her body.

"If you'll just come with me, Miss Larkin." The housekeeper had come in while she was drinking.

"But I am quite warm now and I must..." She looked over her shoulder at Philip as she was borne inexorably away.

"Mrs. Pugh was my nurse," he called after her, as if that explained everything.

Hurry as she might, twenty minutes had passed before she went downstairs again. Her hair, beginning to dry, was fluffing like a black dandelion and she was wearing one of Miss Dorothy's—Lady Vernon's—discarded gowns. Apparently Dorothy Trevelyan had been on the plump side even as a debutante, for the dress hung in folds about Alison. Only a large cashemire shawl lent by Mrs. Pugh made her decent.

Despite the oddity of her attire, she swept into the library and held up her hand imperiously when Philip started to rise from the chair she had rejected.

"No more interruptions," she commanded, standing in front of him. "I came all this way in the rain to tell you something and you will not let me speak a word. Lady Emma has eloped with Ralph Osborne."

"Why are you telling me this?" he asked noncommittally. "Have you decided you want Osborne after all?"

"Certainly not! Because you love Lady Emma!" She was annoyed. "So that you can go after them and persuade her to marry you instead."

"As a matter of fact, I lent them my carriage," he said apologetically.

She stared at him, thunderstruck. "You do not care?"

"Not at all. I am glad for them. It is someone else I love." He pulled her down onto his knee and kissed her.

Surfacing a few minutes later, dazed, breathless and shawl-less, Alison was at a loss for words.

"I'm sorry," Philip said, though now he sounded smug, not apologetic, "I forgot you think kissing is horrid."

"That was quite different from when Lord Kilmore kissed me," she breathed. "Do it again."

He looked at Midnight, blissfully stretched before the fire. The dog's tail thumped twice. So he threw discretion to the winds and obliged.

This time when their lips parted, Alison knew exactly what she wanted to say. Looking up into Philip's dear face, basking in the warmth in his eyes, she said, "I am not precisely sure what a mistress does, but I think I should like to be yours."

"How can I refuse such a handsome offer?" His face was suffused with amusement. "I am honoured to accept, but on one condition: you must marry me first."

"You cannot possibly wish to marry me."

"Why ever not?"

She leaned her head on his shoulder, snugly safe in his arms. "Because you are an important gentleman, a pillar of the establishment."

"A crumbled pillar."

She giggled but persisted. "A gentleman of the first consequence. And I am only a silly girl, dreadfully middle class in spite of Mama. After all, she was only the daughter of a rackety Irish viscount. I would not know how to go on."

"You will learn. You have inherited all the solid, middle class virtues, and someone who can teach herself to read Latin is capable of meeting any challenge. Besides, I could not possibly settle for anything so impermanent as an irregular liaison. A new protector might take you away, and I want you mine forever."

"Really?"

"I have adored you this age. Dare I hope?"

Alison sat up and said with considerable indignation, "You are laughing at me again."

"I can't help it. I never thought to hear a female reject marriage in favour of *carte blanche.*"

"I have not refused."

"You would not accept only because Lord Fane did not come up to scratch?"

"Are you jealous?"

"Yes."

"Lord Fane did come up to scratch. I refused him because I love you so much I could not possibly marry anyone else."

It seemed like the right moment for another kiss.

Some time later, Alison asked dreamily, "Are you sure we have to be married first?"

"Quite sure." Sounding hesitant, Philip went on, "If you really want to be 'your ladyship' I can obtain a title any time, though it will be a little more difficult since my defection. It is just that for three centuries there has been a family tradition of choosing to be commoners."

"Oh no, I never had any desire to be called 'my lady.' I just thought it would be excessively romantic to be loved by a lord. But I have known for some time—" she sighed contentedly "—that nothing in the whole world could possibly be half as romantic as being Mrs. Philip Trevelyan."

This August, don't miss an exclusive
two-in-one collection of earlier love stories

MAN
WITH A PAST

TRUE COLORS

by one of today's hottest
romance authors,

Jayne Ann Krentz

Now, two of Jayne Ann Krentz's most loved books are
available together in this special edition that new and
longtime fans will want to add to their bookshelves.

Let Jayne Ann Krentz capture your hearts with the love
stories, MAN WITH A PAST and TRUE COLORS.

And in October, watch for the second two-in-one
collection by Barbara Delinsky!

Available wherever Harlequin books are sold.

Back by Popular Demand

Janet Dailey
Americana

A romantic tour of America through fifty favorite Harlequin Presents, each set in a different state researched by Janet and her husband, Bill. A journey of a lifetime in one cherished collection.

In July, don't miss the exciting states featured in:

Title #11 — HAWAII
　　　　Kona Winds

　#12 — IDAHO
　　　　The Travelling Kind

*Available wherever
Harlequin books are sold.*